THE SPINNER OF TALES

by Richard Hall

Foreword by Jeffrey Round

ReQueered Tales
Los Angeles • Toronto
2023

The Spinner of Tales

by Richard Hall

First American edition: 2023

This edition: ReQueered Tales, October 2023

ReQueered Tales version 1.20
Kindle edition ASIN: B0CCRFC9YN
Epub edition ISBN-13: 978-1-959902-06-5
Paperback edition ISBN-13: 978-1-959902-07-2
Hardcover edition ISBN-13: 978-1-959902-08-9

*For more information about current and future releases,
please contact us:*
E-mail: *requeeredtales@gmail.com*
Facebook (Like us!): www.facebook.com/ReQueeredTales
Twitter: @ReQueered
Instagram: www.instagram.com/requeered
Web: www.ReQueeredTales.com
Blog: www.ReQueeredTales.com/blog
Mailing list (Subscribe for latest news): https://bit.ly/RQTJoin

Praise for Richard Hall

"There can be no doubt that Hall is indeed a writer
of the first rank."
— *Boston Bay Windows*

"Richard Hall is a true artist, and time will be good
to him. When momentarily more famous writers
are dropped into the trashbin of literary history,
Hall's quality will continue to shine."
— *Chicago Gay Life*

"Hall is, in short, a genius."
— *Baltimore Gay Paper*

"Hall's stories evoke comparison with Henry James
or Maupassant, Hemingway and Fitzgerald ... *Fidelities* is a
luminous collection ... Hall has found in gay life stories to
amuse, entertain, and move."
— *Lambda Book Report*

"*The Butterscotch Prince* is a deliciously written,
softly witty and intricately plotted gay murder mystery ...
A delight!"
— *In Touch*

"*The Butterscotch Prince* has my admiration ...
a good read in one sitting."
— Michael Lynch, *The Body Politic*

By RICHARD HALL

The Butterscotch Prince (1975)

Couplings (1981)

Three Plays for a Gay Theater (1983)

Letter from a Great Uncle (1985)

Family Fictions (1991)

Fidelities (1992)

The Spinner of Tales (2023)

THE SPINNER OF TALES

by Richard Hall

Table of Contents

Richard Hall in Perspective

It is difficult, if not impossible, to look at a writer's first published book and predict what will come next, what territory lies ahead to be explored. Much of that will be dictated by chance and the exigencies of the publishing world – by editors' whims as much as the fickle tastes of critics and readers alike. Who would have thought the slight pieces in Marcel Proust's *Les plaisirs et les jours* would give rise to his monumental *À la recherche du temps perdu* two decades later? Writers must follow their muses if they are to fulfill their promise; what happens afterwards isn't always up to them.

So it was with Richard Hall, who started off writing a piece of would-be pornography, *The Butterscotch Prince*, only to have it rejected for not being up to snuff. It was eventually published two years later, in 1975, as literary fiction. More would follow. Far easier, then, to look at a last work and sum up what has absorbed a writer's attention. This too is true of Hall, a writer who always searched for the perfect form, and whose final work,

RICHARD HALL

The Spinner of Tales, is now published more than thirty years after he died, of AIDS, in 1992. *Spinner*, it turns out, tells us a great deal about where Hall had been.

Intriguingly, Hall wrote (or at least published) in threes: three short story collections (*Couplings, Letter from a Great-Uncle, Fidelities*), three plays (*Happy Birthday, Daddy, Love Match, Prisoner of Love*), three essays (*The Elements of Gay Theater, Gay Theater: Notes from a Diary, The Transparent Closet: Gay Theater for Straight Audiences*), and now, with *The Spinner of Tales*, three novels. It joins *The Butterscotch Prince* and his personal saga, *Family Fictions*.

Hall's themes were shaped by his times. In 1926, the year of his birth, America was at the height of its post-war glory. But it had enjoyed scarcely a decade of that prosperity when it plunged into the Great Depression, and later another world war. Identities were erased wholesale, whether through genocide, the destruction of war, or a pervasive homophobia that discouraged people from being themselves.

Hall was touched by all of these: he was born a Jew, he served in the armed forces, and he was gay. While his early work deals primarily with forging a gay identity, later he dwells on identity more broadly. The dissociation started early. Hall was eight when his mother threw the family into convulsion by changing their name from Hirshfeld to Hall to defend them from growing anti-Semitism. Not satisfied with outward reform, she immersed them in a full religious conversion, from Jewish to Episcopalian, even going so far as to buy New England antiques to outfit their new, fictional heritage.

The experience would become the backbone of *Family Fictions, a crie de coeur* from a writer who spent a lifetime carving out his identity. Nevertheless, he ultimately came to view this second novel in broader terms. In a letter to his younger sister, Marny, in 1991, he wrote, "it is not about the trauma of a changed name or about secret Jewishness, but about ALL secrets ... It is about the strenuous efforts at covering up truth that doesn't fit the prevailing myths."

The search for truth was at the heart of everything Hall wrote and was how he conducted his life as well. It propelled him to come out in the 1940s, when he'd be guaranteed censure, if not outright condemnation. Fortunately, he had a role model, a gay great-uncle with whom he felt a bond. In the Author's Note to *Letter from a Great-Uncle*, he describes how a sex scandal had made the man flee Texas for "exile" in New York. Or perhaps not exile, exactly. In New York, his uncle became "an avid theatergoer" and a manager at Stern Brothers, a department store on 23rd Street, living and eventually dying in the tony Hotel Langwell just off Times Square.

Hall was always intrigued by identity – anyone's. *The Butterscotch Prince* is about two men, one white and the other black, whom the narrator nonetheless considers twins. So, too, in his chilling cautionary tale "Colors", inspired by Conrad's "violently racist" *Heart of Darkness*. Hall was intrigued by Puerto Rico and the tensions in a culture that repressed nonconformist sexuality in some ways but celebrated it in others, as with the spectacle of *las mujeres locas*, men in drag who feature at public festivals for Catholic saints.

Puerto Rico figures in Hall's work almost as much as the search for identity and truth, and it backgrounds many of his short stories. "Prisoner of Love" concerns an uptight PC New Yorker who learns to loosen his morals – at a friend's expense. A fleshedout stage version of "Prisoner" played at The Glines off-Broadway in 1978.

Eric Bentley, writing in the *New York Native*, called Hall's work in theater "outstanding."

For Hall, Puerto Rico is a crucible, home to some but a prison to others, as well as a Shangri-La, leaving which means destruction. It is both a land of bright promise and dark despair and, sometimes, against all odds, a paradise regained. He knew the culture well, having taught at the island's Inter American University, a private Christian college. Tellingly, he set his reimagining of Thomas Mann's *Death in Venice* there, titling it "Death in San Juan." As with "Colors", Hall ends the story with a twist that reclaims classic literature for queer readers in order to "undo some evasion or injustice in the original."

His 1981 short story collection, *Couplings*, features three such works, along with a note that he had concluded the project. Nevertheless, a spectacular fourth, "Country People," inspired by EM Forster's "Doctor Woolacott", appeared in his final collection, *Fidelities*, in 1992. Hall had reviewed Forster's posthumous *The Life to Come*, calling some of its stories masterpieces. Clearly inspired by the work, "Country People" is not so much an updating of Forster as a reinvention that far surpasses it. It would win a posthumous Gaylactic Spectrum Award in 2005. In 2021 it became an award-winning short film by writer and director David Bobrow.

Though he kept an eye on contemporary trends, Hall looked uneasily to posterity. In an essay commissioned by guest editor Ian Young for *Little Caesar 12*, Dennis Cooper's anarcho-punk literary journal, Hall wrote a tribute to the Jewish-American author Edward Lewis Wallant, whose work disappeared from view soon after he died at 36. Listing reasons for Wallant's neglect, Hall cited his early passing, his minimal output and the failure of his work to sustain critical interest after his death. He had "been buried in the ceaseless tide of newer writers, newer books." Although Hall lived thirty years longer than Wallant, he might well have been writing his own epitaph. Despite ranking with the rising tide of gay writers of his generation, including the famed Violet Quill, he has suffered similar neglect.

A testament to Hall's talent is that little in his work dates it. At his best he writes with an enviable precision and depth of feeling. His characters are fully alive. The prejudices and ills he tackles, even those we might have presumed dead and buried ages ago, are still with us. In the play *Happy Birthday, Daddy*, a man leaves his family for another man and finds himself at the opposite end of a teeter-totter from his scandalized teenage son. "Country People" reaches across generations to lay its ghostly hands on all plagues, past, present and future.

Hall's endings often turn on a dime, with insights that dazzle and liberate his characters from the weight of the past. They open doors and mark exits where none seemed to be. The very best of his work, in particular the later short stories, stand with those of contemporaries like Ethan Canin and William Trevor, who also wrote about the search for truth and identity, though not from a gay perspective. Hall would have liked the comparison. While he defined and wrote for a gay audience, his aim was always to supersede whatever limitations categories imposed on writing.

Puerto Rico makes a final, spectacular comeback in *The Spinner of Tales*, about the murder of Miles Halloran, a dancer turned gothic-romance writer turned sculptor. Miles had drifted through life, but the one thing he excelled at was inventing stories, even if he sometimes found it hard to distinguish between fact and fantasy. His friend, Bruce Pittman, an HIV+ music teacher with his time running out, pushes for the truth, knowing in the end that truth is all we have. *Spinner* is very much a novel of its time, yet one that reaches out to ours as well.

As with *The Butterscotch Prince*, this last novel is a mystery, the two titles tidily bookending Hall's career. While outwardly similar, they are decidedly different in scope and technique. Each searches for gay identity via a bond formed between two men and each culminates in an historic LGBTQ event – in the first an early Pride march, in the second an early AIDS march – that tracks the turn from optimism to despair and eventually to rage. Otherwise, they are worlds apart. While *The Butterscotch Prince* seems to have been written as a Look-What-I-Can-Do lark, *The Spinner of Tales* is serious fiction. Here, the tentative groping for identity in the first book is replaced by an ardent, hard-won acceptance of that identity. *Spinner* doesn't rival Hall's earlier achievements so much as it neatly sums them up.

Toward the end of his life, when his sister Marny complained that she wasn't really gifted like him, Hall commiserated, saying everyone felt that way about someone else. In his case, it was Forster. Both writers, having achieved prominence in their lifetime, left behind unpublished works. But where Forster suppressed one of his best novels, *Maurice*, fearing in early days that its themes might damage his reputation then later concluding it wasn't worth publishing, Hall had no desire to hold anything back. He had always stood for truth.

In 1992, as he struggled to put all his talent into a final, frenzied send-off, Marny warned him the effort would kill him. She was right. The day her beloved brother typed THE END on the manuscript of *The Spinner of Tales*, he unplugged his feeding tube and entered hospice, where he died a week later. He had instructed her to give the finished manuscript to his agent – who was already sick himself and could not take it on.

The Spinner of Tales sat with Marny Hall for more than thirty years. She has now placed her brother's last words in the right hands, those of ReQueered Tales and posterity as well. Let this not be the last brick on Richard Hall's tomb, however. Rather, let it be a crowning achievement that signals his long-overdue return from the shadows. Together let us celebrate this remarkable conclusion to his life and rediscover the wonders of his work.

Jeffrey Round
Toronto,
February, 2023

Jeffrey Round is an award-winning author, filmmaker, and songwriter. His breakout novel, *A Cage of Bones*, was listed on AfterElton's 50 Best Gay Books. *Lake on the Mountain*, first of the seven Dan Sharp mysteries, won a Lambda Award in 2013. His latest book is the poetry collection *Threads* (2022) from Beautiful Dreamer Press.

For Harold Westphal

I dreamed about Miles Halloran again last night – not as he was in the hour of his violent death, but as he appeared at the start of our friendship, when I spotted him on that overheated beach in Puerto Rico. In my dream, he had that quality of specialness that had attracted me at once. The other sunbathers might have seen a tall man, well into middle age, with a too slender body, hair of relentless gold and a manner best described as all-points-alert, but I saw someone else. Someone who wasn't afraid to be stared and giggled at, who was inviolate in his self-esteem, who had clearly lived many lives in many places.

In the dream, we stood again at the thatched hut where they sold soft drinks and rancid chicken and watched a young man doing gymnastics for the benefit of his girlfriend. And once again, Miles remarked, "He's courting her with cartwheels, he's rolling over her heart with his feet in the air and his palms on the ground." And once again I laughed and decided this outrageous personage was someone I wanted to know better.

The dream ended, as all dreams do, before it had really finished. I reflected that whoever planted the dreaming capacity in us had a rotten sense of form. Miles would have done better – he rarely left a tale unfinished and if you complained he'd finish it for you on the spot. But then, he was a professional spinner of tales. The only story for which he couldn't find the perfect ending was his own.

But I'm getting ahead of my tale, which Miles never did. I will begin at the beginning.

1

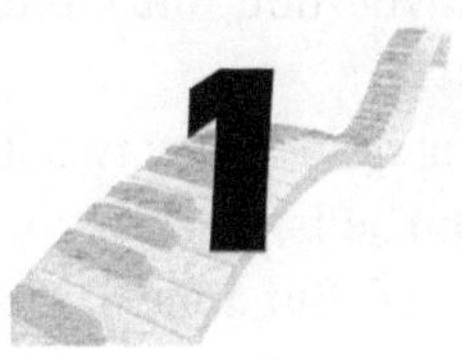

I'M NOT THE EXCITABLE TYPE, which has certain advantages if you're a music teacher. Student frustration, discouragement – not to mention hysteria and tantrums – don't get very far. You smile and refuse to get involved. This is like leaving a partner alone on the dance floor.

On the other hand, too much phlegm restricts your responses. You don't soar with the good students, thrill with the great ones. "Oh, Dr. Pittman, you never say anything nice," is a complaint I hear a lot. Or, from the older students, "Come on, Bruce, that slow movement was good and you know it."

And so I waver between the limited poles of my temperament (from "okay" to "could be better"), and wish I were different. More tempest-tossed, more savage. But it isn't to be, any more than I will perform at Carnegie Hall. The day I turned thirty, looked in the mirror and saw I had lost more than half my hair, that my shoulders had started a downward slope that nothing could arrest, that my hands, though large and sinewy, were hung from bean-pole arms, and that the general effect was of a pale, good-natured bat suffering from mild acromegaly – on that day, I began the process of self-acceptance that has kept me steady for the last fifteen years. This is the way I am. This is how Doctor Bruce Pittman (Ph.D. Piano, Juilliard) looks. Maybe God put me together in a fit of absent-mindedness.

I went the other route in my twenties, of course, like everybody else. Barbells, chest expanders, push-ups. Nautilus and Universal. But none of these efforts brought my shy muscles to the surface, and I didn't have much free time to keep at it. No, my sinews lay buried under the surface of my pinkish skin; the definition I sought remained elusive. It seemed that people liked my face – trusted it – but gave only passing attention to the rest of me. I recalled a description of Aldous Huxley in a bathing suit – all mind and no body. An anatomical impossibility, but I understood what D.H. Lawrence meant when he made the crack.

§ § §

Not that I abdicated from the sexual marketplace, not in New York in the 1970s, when the city reeked of freedom. Of course, my appearance in a bar or sauna didn't set off a stampede. But there is someone for everyone, just as there is a bug for every vegetable, and I always came out okay. More than okay – at least twice with a connection that lasted half a decade or more and contradicted everything I'd been taught to expect in the bitter lees of my adolescence. Maybe these partners (*lovers* is the wrong word – too excitable) liked my quietudes. Maybe they appreciated the fact that I got up every morning at eight, practiced for two hours, then went to a settlement school where I taught beautiful kids for the rest of the day. Maybe they extended their trust in my face to trust in something else – in themselves or their future. But Hector Armendariz, who was from Santo Domingo, and Timothy Currier, who was from Maine, gave me, one at a time, all they had. Eventually we used it up – there seems to be a limit to what can be passed between two partners of any gender combination – and we had to part. It was no one's fault; it was foretold in our flesh, in our respective histories, in the nature of time itself. Not that it happened without breaking and tearing, without awful midnights when I rolled around my double bed in the loft on 18th Street like a creature in a painting by Bosch. I remember walking around the West Side of Manhattan in a state of confusion bordering on hallucination, playing over and over in my mind the first Prelude and Fugue of Book I, convinced that the right fingering, the correct digital sequence, would firm up my place in the universe. Would, in fact, locate the universe itself, which had been giving clear signs of slipping out of my grasp forever. But eventually, new habits, or new resignations, asserted themselves, and I survived.

And there was always music, therapy without end, my own twelve-note program. When I couldn't use it spiritually I used it technically, scales and arpeggios for hours, and when that failed I used it clerically. Yes, I sat down with score paper, ruler and French curve and wrote out whole movements of Beethoven sonatas, Bach fugues, Chopin ballades, from memory. This calmed me. I recalled that Talleyrand, in prison, had thrown a box of pins on the floor of his black cage every morning, then spent the rest of the day groping for them. He said later that counting the pins had saved his sanity. Copying music, at certain times, was my box of pins.

Maybe I should use the rest of this introductory space to discuss New Jersey. It isn't everyone who will admit to coming from there – a state without a soul, as they say of Argentina – but I was born in Red Bank, so there you are. My mother drove my father out by the time I was seven, a departure for which I never blamed him after I got a clear fix on my mother. Except for occasional letters and one memorable summer in Bakersfield I had little to do with him. When I asked why he left us, he always said the same thing. "Ask your mother." I knew better than to do that.

Roberta – I never called her anything else once I got past the sucking sounds that spelled Mama – was a natural jailer, the world a dungeon she had been put in charge of. She never wavered. Because she had answers, people gravitated to her, women and men, pushing against her certitudes like plastic wrap against marble. The more I listened to her opinions, her formulas, the more sure I became that I didn't want a life filled with answers. Questions were more my style. When I discovered the piano, I turned it into a giant question machine. Schubert's song, *Die Neugierige*, became my theme song. Every cadence became a way of expressing uncertainty. And when I wasn't playing, I was reading – once again focusing on questions, not answers.

Just the two of us – it sounds like the title of a British road comedy – but it's a statement full of limitation. Where were the others? The uncles and aunts and grandparents and cousins? Aside from that lone man in Bakersfield, my ex-father, there was nobody. They were either dead or had never existed. And so I grew skilled at reading my mother's moods. I learned the semiotics of gesture – the purse of the lips, the angle of the elbow, the flick of the eyelash, the slight flare of the nostrils. This would eventually prove useful with students but at the time, sharing that small house on Pennyfeather Road, my survival depended on an accurate reading of her secret signs. Part of my technique was not to get excited. My excitement was like a drug to my mother. It made her quiver with pleasure at the arguments to come, as if she were rehearsing for the local groups which she organized and directed – the PTA, Mothers Against Drunk Driving, The Permanent Voter Registration Drive, Women Against Pornography. Finally, after leaving home for Juilliard and a life for which I was barely fitted at first, I realized that I had learned all the survival skills I needed from my mother. We had been lost in a wilderness together – the wilderness of growing up – and I could manage better than I thought, once I found my way out.

One last note about Roberta. She was a genius at the stock market. Don't ask me why – its disciplines, perversities, variations, were not suited to her temperament, which was angry and straightforward. But there was some unglimpsed patience in her, some slyness and deferral of gratification that made the irrationalities of the market clear. She liked to say it was horse racing for college graduates but she didn't really mean that.

She kept her doings a secret from me, but I knew where the transaction slips were – in the locked metal box at the top of her closet. Once I found the key (in an old handbag), I made it my business to keep tabs. Not that I gloated or got excited. It was just one question more: why was she getting rich without telling anyone?

But that's why, when Roberta died six years ago, I was able, in partnership with Luddie Chametsky, to buy the ailing Longacre Music School on Charles Street. Of course, she died intestate, as if she had no heir, which delayed things for more than a year and constituted the final, unanswerable question: *Who did she think I was?*

§ § §

Dr. Zinsser was not the punctual sort. Not because he was inconsiderate of his patients or burdened with an incompetent staff but because the hours didn't register. When God gave him a sense of space, the other a priori, time, was omitted. For Dr. Z, everything happened more or less at once, in a primeval chaos. The rest of us knew that time had been invented to keep events from occurring simultaneously, but this news hadn't reached the good doctor.

There were four of us in his office that Tuesday afternoon. A man in his early thirties in a business suit, an attaché case at his feet, with perfectly chiseled features, who was obviously intended to be the next Secretary of Treasury. Also a sweet-faced young man wearing wire rims, his skin the color of cocoa butter, who was trading remarks with Harvey, the office nurse/factotum. And a talkative young man, in his late twenties, who was telling me about the buddy facilities at New York University – Bellevue. "Two beds in every room," he said, "you can have your lover stay overnight, wheel you down to the cafeteria, hold your hand during chemo, whatever." He was spotted with lesions here and there – purple medallions, the new leprosy – but his voice was bright. "A lotta people say First Avenue is too far over, but what is it, a crosstown bus? Ten minutes, you're there."

His name was Vinnie, a blond Italian, I thought. As he talked, he whittled at a bar of soap. A woman's head was emerging – frizzed, with Afro curls. I recalled Michelangelo's Chained Slave. This woman was caught in her soap like the slave in stone.

I figured I had at least an hour to wait, maybe more.

The door to the inside office opened and a Hispanic woman, middle-aged, came out. She was heavy set, with sea-green eyes. From each ear dangled a gold earring depicting the crucified Christ. Both Christ figures had their eyes wide open, checking us out. She called a thank you to the doctor, invisible inside, and headed for Harvey's desk to pay. I don't know what I expected – stereotypes are hard to shake – but she produced a personalized check, not a Medicaid card. I could see, on the check, palm trees and a sunset. She paid the fee without a word.

Zinsser appeared at the door, looking somewhat better than three months ago. Then he had told me he was going to take a vacation in Europe. It had obviously helped. His eyes looked less bloodshot, the capillaries in his cheeks no longer pink spiderwebs. He looked almost healthy, a remarkable achievement considering that he'd been coping with the health crisis for a dozen years and had watched hundreds of his patients die.

Vinnie, the Michelangelo of soap, was next. I noticed he wasn't wearing his shoes. The door closed behind him. I picked up a year-old copy of *People*.

My last piano lesson, just before coming here, had been with Emily Warshow, who had been giving signs of rebelliousness recently. Not that I minded – temperament was to be encouraged. But Emily's revolt was not due to the music she was studying. Her boyfriend had been arrested on a drug charge; he dealt out of an expensive apartment house on 14th Street. "There are two ways to play this Scarlatti, Emily," I had said, my voice resolutely neutral. "One way is lyrical, which is romantic and nineteenth century. Another is like a guitar which is probably how Scarlatti played it, since he lived in Spain most of his life." I paused, as another idea took shape. "Or you might find the sadness, the melancholy. It's there, under the bursts of melody. But you can't play it like a machine gun. Nobody ever wrote sonatas for machine guns."

She didn't like that at all. She slammed the Kalmus edition shut, said she wasn't genetically programmed for the 18th century and opened the Alban Berg sonata. We spent the rest of the hour trying to tone that down.

I sighed. I had quit teaching at three today – a six-hour day, half of it spent on general school duties, dealing with staff, with Luddie. Nothing new. But when I left to keep this appointment, I had to take a cab. The walk, once so pleasurable, between Charles and East 19th Street, was no longer possible. Another little defeat. I turned to stare out the window – a courtyard filled with trash. No use thinking about it. Besides, Dr. Zinsser might have something new. Finally the door opened and Vinnie padded out, grinning. I wondered if I would be smiling in his place. He sat in the chair he had vacated, reached under, and took out some shoe skates, the old kind with four wheels in a square. He put them on, then skated over to Harvey. A Medicaid card was produced. When he was done, he turned to grin at the rest of us. "Guess I'll roll on home," he said. We could hear the wheels on the tiles of the hall outside. They sounded like rain on a tin roof.

It was five before I got inside – a wait of medium length. "How are you feeling?" A casual inflection but soft brown eyes scanned me. I spoke of my shortness of breath, my increased fatigue. He had me strip, took weight and blood pressure. My T-4 cells had slipped some more; other ratios were less encouraging. We discussed various therapies and dosages. My recent X-rays were dubious. He thought I should have a bronchoscopy. Next week maybe?

I agreed. Then he squared off his controlled-substance form. I could have anything I wanted – Librium,

Valium, Xanax, Prozac, Ativan, Elavil. A junky's dream. I refused them all. "I'll just try to keep working," I said. "That's the best tranquilizer."

He nodded. "I don't want you to think of yourself as sick, Bruce. Do everything you normally do."

I thought briefly of the mornings when I could hardly get out of bed. When the least exertion set me coughing. When the mild stresses and strains of school took on hurricane proportions. When I had to close my office door for a quick nap. When do you think of yourself as sick – when you've got an IV drip in your arm and a respirator down your throat? But I didn't complain. Dr. Zinsser was being psychological and his words, despite their illogic, made me feel better.

I determined to walk home to Twelfth Street, stopping first for coffee and pastry for a sugar rush. I wouldn't make it otherwise. It was a warm September evening, and the street scene was inspiring. I passed young men in denims and tank tops, in walking shorts and all-American Boy muscle shirts. A spasm of nostalgia raced through me – all this sexual display had meant something once, a golden promise that was the essence of living downtown. But now ...

I blinked, rubbed my eyes. Several of the handsome young men on the street were carrying something on their backs. It was small, carried high between the shoulders. I stared at each as he passed. Nausea rose in me, followed by terror. I was hallucinating. I had seen something I shouldn't see. On each of those backs, visible only to me, was a death.

I hurried home, hardly raising my eyes from the pavement until I fitted my key into my front-door lock.

The summer evening was going into its final dark, almost nine, when I woke up. I had been aware of the phone ringing in the other room, the machine clicking several times, but it was impossible to struggle up out of my dream. My sleep had a different quality these days – deeper, more tidal, pulling me to new oblivion. And when I came out, I was frequently exhausted, for reasons unknown.

I played back my messages – a few from Erica, my secretary at school, one from the president of this co-op about joining the Finance Committee, another from my downstairs neighbor complaining about the music last night. She had an invalid husband and two unmusical cats. Last night there had been a birthday party here for Luddie Chametsky Jr., just turned ten. With a musical crowd, what did Mrs. Marranca expect? Quiet conversation?

The machine switched off and I went to the piano, dribbling a few chords quietly. I recalled my hallucinations on the street. They seemed absurd now, the result of two obsessive hours in the doctor's office, the smell of doom all around. My fingers – both hands now – pressed out the lumpy progressions of a Brahms intermezzo. I tried not to think.

The ringing phone was a blessed reprieve. I jumped up and crossed the room. It was David Donnenfeld, just back from his Mexico tour. I couldn't have asked for a better antidote. "David! You're back!"

"Late last night." The low, pleasing tone of his voice, always calm and unruffled, soothed me instantly. David, my star pupil, the Longacre Music School's chief claim to fame, and a fixture in our advertisements ("Among our graduates are David Donnenfeld and Shirley Scott ...").

"How did it go?"

"The tour? Not bad."

Another pleasing quality – he never hyped himself,

never indulged in false animation. "You played at Bellas Artes?"

A chuckle. "I saw the famous glass curtain. The volcanoes. I thought if I played the Liszt they might shatter but they didn't." Another chuckle, then a pause. "How do you feel, Bruce?"

A flurry of replies went through my head. Brave. Dismissive. Self-pitying. I waited till a good one floated to the surface. "Not so hot, David."

"I brought you something from Mexico City. What are you doing?"

"You mean now?"

"Yeah."

"Outlining my obituary."

The laughter that followed freed us both. "Well, I have some ideas on that. Can I come over?"

I promised to put coffee on and hung up. David Donnenfeld was the right person for now. I could feel old, time-honored illusions thronging around me. I had been a little in love with David at one time – despite, or because of, the age difference.

Plugging in the coffee maker, I thought about my initial encounter with him during the school's first year of operation. He'd walked into the downstairs office in the middle of a minor crisis. Fiona McCleary, one of our piano instructors, student of Tobias Matthay and Myra Hess, keeper of the high British flame of pianism ("I want them to study Beethoven, there is nothing that cures American *messiness* like Beethoven") was having a fight. Not with me but with Erica, my secretary. "But my dear girl," Fiona fumed, her plaid, round-the-shoulder scarf heaving on her chest, "I was waiting upstairs the whole time, why didn't you send him up?"

Erica's face crumpled. "Miss McCleary, I didn't see

you come in, I didn't know you were up there."

"You didn't see me come in?" Fiona's voice turned baritone. When angry she produced testosterone. "You didn't see *me*?"

"Oh God." Erica, usually so tough, couldn't deal with outraged Albion. I stepped out of my sanctum.

"Dr. Pittman," Fiona pronounced my title as if it were an unforgivable lapse of taste. "Your secretary has sent away my two o'clock student, a young man I expressly wanted to see, who had prepared the Marche Funèbre sonata for today, because she thought I was not on the premises." She paused, her pale face glowing like a malevolent moon. "I expect the school to pay my fee anyway. I can't come all the way from Cliffside to find my lessons canceled through inattention."

Erica snatched her purse from her desk and headed for the Ladies'. At that moment the door opened and a slender young man appeared. He looked from Fiona to me and back again, trying to figure out who was in charge. His skin was pale, his eyes large and dark; he seemed to quiver all over like an arrow arrested in flight. "I … I wanted to see about taking one of your piano courses," he stammered. He looked at Fiona.

She turned the full light of her countenance on him. "Young man, you have come to the wrong school. This one is hopelessly mismanaged."

He quivered some more. I had ten seconds to keep him on the premises. "If you'll just have a seat over there," I said in my least excitable tone, "I'll be with you in a moment." Clutching a briefcase, he settled down. I turned to Fiona, my mind snapping into a familiar groove. I had my usual reaction to bullying; it reminded me of Red Bank and Roberta. "I'm sorry, Fiona, I'm not convinced that Erica saw you go upstairs. It was an honest mistake.

Under the circumstances, we'll pay you half the lesson fee."

It occurred to me that a new student shouldn't be hearing this squabble. Glancing his way I saw his eyes enlarge even more. I turned back to Fiona. She had retreated. "I'm not sure I can accept that."

I nodded. She'd given in. I pointed to the schedule on the bulletin board. "Your three o'clock student has been waiting ten minutes now. If you're not careful you'll lose her too."

With a last protest she turned and left. A noble exit, like that of the Marschallin in Act III. I turned to the newcomer. He was 19, he said, and his name was David Donnenfeld. He had planned to go to Juilliard, but since he lived on Grove Street, just a block away, and worked as a waiter at Chumley's around the corner, he thought it would be more convenient to study here. Besides, his friend Miles Halloran had recommended us. I invited him into my office, where I kept the enrollment forms, making a note to call Miles and thank him. This wasn't the first favor he had done us.

Of course, I had to audition the newcomer. Not that we turned anyone away in those days but there was the matter of placement. After I took down the essential information (born in Brooklyn, father deceased, mother a retired pieceworker in the ILGWU, older brother a dentist, younger sister married, a succession of piano teachers in and around Eastern Parkway), I thought I had the picture. He belonged in Grade II – second year. That probably meant Fiona and heaps of Beethoven. I motioned to his briefcase. "Can you play for me now?"

He followed me to the second floor auditorium where we kept the Bechstein, our most precious possession. I expected him to open the briefcase and take something out – a Schubert impromptu or, God help us, *Für Elise*, but the suitcase stayed on the floor. He sat on the padded stool and twiddled the elevation knobs – rather expertly, I thought. "What do you want me to play?"

"Whatever you like, David."

Something flamed in the air between us. I tensed, ready for a surprise. He leaned forward, prepared, and began the Beethoven Opus 110, the next-to-last sonata, one of the ground breakers in the literature. It was almost like hearing the piece for the first time, though I spotted some structural deficiencies, some unconvincing tempi, some niggling contrasts, some muddiness in the fugue. Still, I sat transfixed until the final swing back to A-flat. When he finished he took his hands off the keys and sat staring. All the tension was gone from his shoulders, torso. A looseness, almost a rubbery quality, had transformed him. I thought briefly of Liszt, whom contemporaries claimed had no muscles in his hands and arms, who simply oozed into the keyboard like ectoplasm. What kind of gift was this? Where had it come from? The ability to move instantly behind the notes, to find the secret poetry most pianists spend a lifetime looking for – how had this young man from Brooklyn managed?

"You must have had good teachers, David."

He turned toward me, smiling. His teeth were large and even. I thought of his brother, the dentist. "They were okay." He shrugged. "Nothing special. I don't think they really knew what to do with me."

"They must have taught you something."

"I think I upset them. It never took me that long to memorize a piece."

I gestured to his briefcase. "You have a pretty big repertory?"

"Oh, those are books in there. Stuff I'm reading."

Later, when we started lessons (yes, I elected myself his instructor), I found that he had drastically understated his powers of memory. He didn't carry music around in a briefcase because it leaped, more or less, from the page into his auditory memory without the necessity of practice. I had never come across a facility like this before. It was part visual acuity, part auditory imprinting, part magic. It seemed that David Donnenfeld had been receiving music from the age of three, when he had hoisted himself to the family upright and only left it when forced to. As we continued talking that first afternoon, I felt the surge of an old idea of mine – *reincarnation*. How else to explain gifts like these, if not as the reappearance of old souls? Nothing else really fit the facts, though whenever I broached this perfectly logical idea, people looked at me as if I'd just asked for their astrological signs.

My doorbell rang thirty minutes later. David's face against mine was cool. I inhaled icy fragrances, felt the sandpapery surface of his cheek. He had to shave a second time before concerts. His arms were hard and wiry around me.

He reared back to examine me. "I see signs of advanced decay."

"You bastard."

"What you need is to teach less and supervise more. How's Fiona?"

"Fiona is the same. She asked about you the other day. She brags about you to her new students."

He had brought me a present. A tape, surreptitiously made during Callas's *Bellas Artes* recital in Mexico City in 1952. He handed it over with glee. "There's a high E-flat in the Mad Scene. I heard it's the last one she ever hit."

I gave him another hug, then went for the coffee.

I could hear him diddling at the piano. Maybe later he'd play. He liked to try out repertory on me – not that he needed my comments nowadays.

When I returned, he had moved to the couch. Silence prevailed for a long minute – the good kind that clears away trivia.

"So," he said at last.

"So," I repeated, aware that in feeling free to tell David anything at all, I had eliminated the need. The street scene, the death packets, my narcolepsy and budding depression – all that could be skipped. They had lost their power to harm. One person, I thought, you only need one person, and the world alters. David had been that person for almost ten years now.

He had moved from gifted amateur to full professional within three years of coming to Longacre. It had been mostly a matter of clearing away the eccentricities, then watching him take off. At times, foolishly, I tried to take credit, but I knew I had little to do with it. He would have bloomed with any teacher.

I suppose there is always love between special students and susceptible teachers, but David and I limited its expression. There was no sex between us, though sometimes I ached to strip him of his clothes, to examine that hard, thin body patched with occasional hair, to absorb the mysterious emanations of his talent through my fingertips, tongue, cock, toes. But I never did, though there were times, at the keyboard, when he would lean toward me and I knew the next move was up to me. But I held back, even one afternoon in his little flat on Grove Street, when he pulled me onto his bed and kissed me. We lay there, hearts pounding, parts tingling, on the verge of changing our boundaries for good – but we didn't. Maybe we were both afraid. Maybe we knew, in some old instinctive part of ourselves, that boundaries were useful and shouldn't be abandoned. Maybe we understood that music defined us more accurately than romance ever could. But we drew apart, burst out laughing, gave each other a wild grope and rearranged our clothes. In a way we had made love – and that particular tension between us disappeared for good.

David was still sitting on the couch, waiting for me to end our easy silence. I looked at him carefully. He was 28 now, and had filled out in the last year or two. No longer slender and delicate, no longer quivering. His face was fuller, his hands broader, his shoulders more muscular. A new solidity was settling on him, though the quicksilver came back at the keyboard.

"I went to see Zinsser today," I began. "He's my doctor. He wants me to go to St. Vincent's for a few days."

"I see." He sipped his coffee. No trace of surprise.

"Tests mostly. A bronchoscopy, to see if they can find out what's causing my breathing problems."

"I thought you had that beat with aerosol pentamidine."

I shook my head. "Not working so well. I don't know what they expect to find."

He wouldn't let me off the hook. "Things can grow in your lungs. KS. TB. MAI."

I nodded. "Better to find out as soon as possible, then you can prophylax for it." The medical jargon slid off my lips. We were all experts these days.

"How do you feel about all that?"

I tried to laugh but it came out fake. "They can probably keep me alive for a while."

"Maybe long enough to be cured."

I knew about that – the buy-time theory. My face must have registered contempt because he continued.

"On the other hand, you might go down pretty fast."

"Especially with the pneumonia. It's explosive." I shrugged and adduced the most useful cliché in American life. "At this point, I'm trying to take it one day at a time." The words left my lips with a little pop, like a soda can opening. David stared at me; those dark wide-angle lenses took it all in.

And then, suddenly, it was time to change the subject. "Why don't you play something?" I asked.

He waited a moment, and I could almost see his spirit slipping into a new groove. "What do you want me to play?"

"Whatever you like, David."

We both smiled. It was an old joke now – his first audition at the Bechstein, when I had expected him to play *Für Elise*. Before getting up he reached over and touched my hand, pressing his fingers into the flesh above my thumb, massaging me for a moment. The transmission of touch, of grace. Then he got up and went to the piano.

He played Scott Joplin. The rags didn't sound perky and whorehouse. On the contrary, they sounded sad and silvery and elegant. I thought first of a New Orleans jazz funeral and then my mind slipped a cog and I imagined that Schubert had turned his peasant waltzes, his Ländler, into a set of modern elegies.

After that he played Grieg, the Lyric Suite. Maybe he wanted to finish with something cheerful. At the end I glimpsed young brides, their heads crowned with braids, dancing around the men while reindeer pawed the snow. I had played that piece in Red Bank – it was my mother's favorite, the only one that could lure her to sit down and listen. She invariably applauded when I finished. As I did now. After that we talked about David's Central American tour just concluded, and his upcoming swing through

Canada. Before leaving he kissed me smack on the lips – a gesture with a defiant message all its own.

After he left I put on the Callas tape, but I fell asleep in the middle of the *Casta Diva* – never my favorite aria. At the last moment, between waking and sleeping, when her coarse, intense tones had blended into a pitchless blur, I heard myself mumble aloud, "I don't know, David, I don't know." But what it was I didn't know, I can't say, because the next instant I was sound asleep.

S T. VINCENT'S HOSPITAL ON WEST 11th Street is staffed by nurses, mostly Irish and Italian, who are supervised by pale, winged creatures called Sisters. These angels glide through the corridors on crepe soles and peer at patients with God-haunted eyes. The rest of the time, I believe, they spend in the hospital's rococo chapel praying for victory over Satan, dust, infection and malpractice suits.

The attendant who flipped me onto a tea cart and trundled me up to surgery also brought me down an hour later. "That wasn't so bad, was it?" he asked. Professional cheer, a conspiracy to deny pain, I thought, and if I'd been able to speak – my larynx was too sore for that – I would have disagreed. I reminded myself to tell him later that I didn't mind having a tube run up my nose and down my throat but I hated being told it was nothing.

The verdict was delivered by a resident named Dr. Marshall later the same day, while Angela Michaels was sitting by my bed. "Bruce, we found a low-grade infection in your lower lobar region. A touch of PCP. Antibiotics will fix it."

"See, there's nothing to worry about," Angela chimed in.

More false cheer. What was it about hospitals that turned everyone into bearers of disinformation? I turned toward Angela. "Nothing to worry about unless I want to live more than a year." My voice was still croaky.

"Now, now," Dr. Marshall put in, taking a Charm from her pocket, unwrapping it and popping it in her mouth. "We have some very effective drugs."

She named several. They sounded like science-fiction titles. The Seven Moons of Septra. The Ant-People of Dapsone. The Prophecies of Clindamycin. I would take Septra intravenously for 24 hours. After that I would go home and pop it in pill form.

We discussed allergenic reactions to the IV – nothing to worry about there either, staff standing by to prevent anaphylactic shock. She winked at me when she said this. Obviously I was being treated to the private lingo of the trade, a sign of esteem. Finally I nodded and she left, secure in my acquiescence.

I know why hospitals brought out an old, ugly side of me. It wasn't just the pain and indignity of tubes and syringes and taps, it was the humiliation of having your body treated like a piece of meat. You check something precious at the door of any hospital – yourself. You're reduced to a set of entrails and ganglia, bowel movements and wounds. I used to hate being sick at home with my mother – it increased her power over me ten-fold. And here I was, pinned to a bed while two nurses wheeled in the IV apparatus. One nurse held my forearm, the other kept a blood pressure gauge in place as she inserted the needle in the back of my hand, taped it tightly, observed the life-giving ichor flowing into my veins.

"Well now, that wasn't so bad, was it?" she chirped.

I had a sudden idea for a hospital cantata – choruses of health-care workers singing that line in a five-part fugue.

"It was okay," I murmured.

"Now your friend can sit here again."

Angela continued dispensing her particular brand of optimism. "Bruce dear, you're lucky to be in St. Vincent's. I spent three weeks here when I had my radical, and they couldn't have been nicer."

Her voice rose slightly. Her face, once slender but now, in her late forties, round and slightly jowly, beamed with good will. It was true – she had spent three awful weeks here while they cut off her left breast, some years back. But she had survived. What did I have to complain about? Yet.

"Now I want you to work on some positive imaging. You know what that is?"

I shook my head.

"They have a lady who comes around three days a week and teaches it. It's a mind-control thing."

I groaned. I might have known.

Angela rummaged in her tote bag. "I also brought you something from Integral Yoga." She cast a look at the door. "I know you're not supposed to eat anything from outside." She took out some small objects. They looked like shrunken human heads. "Shiitake mushrooms," she said, "dynamite for the immune system. They cost eighteen dollars a pound. I could only afford three." She looked around again. "I'll slip them in the drawer here. You nibble on them when you feel like it." I closed my eyes, hearing the drawer in the nightstand open and close. When I opened them again, Angela was sitting demurely, smoothing her skirt. Supervisor Sister had just glided in and was looking at us suspiciously. "Gifts of food are not encouraged," she said.

"I know that, Sister."

A pause. Maybe it was against their creed to catch someone in a lie. A nod and she glided off. Angela put her hand over her mouth. A school kid who had just evaded punishment. I had to laugh – my first laugh of the past few days. "Angela," I said, "who gives the best hug in the world?"

It was an old joke. She stood up. "I do, you silly twerp." She proceeded to demonstrate her talent. It was a little tricky with the IV stand, the slithery feed lines, my prone position, but she managed. Her face against mine smelled of cucumber soap – she was addicted to vegetable cleansing agents. A wave of sensuality went through me. I wasn't ready to give up the smells of the world, not by a long shot.

"Did you bring some music?" she asked, disengaging.

I pointed to my Walkman and a pile of tapes.

"When you're tired of those, I'll bring some of my own."

Angela had a gorgeous alto voice and soloed regularly at churches around town. She had also given a couple of song recitals. She was especially notable for her Schumann – *Der Nussbaum* could break your heart. After one of her church solos, I had been introduced by mutual friends. After that, music kept us together.

"I have to go now," she whispered, "I have an audition."

Another chaste kiss on my forehead. She turned. That's when I noticed it. "Angela!"

She stopped, swiveled her head slowly around "Ye-e-e-e-s?"

"What's that?"

She giggled. "That's my mouse tail. I thought you'd get a kick out of it." She reached down and touched the wiry grey fabric dropping below the hem of her skirt.

I began to laugh. She looked deliriously happy. "It's from my days in the Wicca coven. The mouse was my totem animal."

My lungs hurt from laughing.

"I didn't mind most of it but walking through the park at dawn on the summer solstice was too much. We might have been killed." She batted her eyes. "I guess you could call me a recovering witch."

And she was gone.

I slept for a while, the Valium still working in my veins. It was a pleasant sleep, inside a soft white haze. When I came out of it, Miles Halloran was standing in the doorway. It was late in the afternoon. He arched an eyebrow under his henna pompadour and brought forth a nosegay of violets. "I came to see if you're still alive," he said.

I motioned him in, and he oozed forward in an eel-like motion. Yet he was surprisingly graceful. He had been a dancer in *The Red Shoes*. He was British by birth.

He peered down at me. "Not dead yet?"

"No."

He sighed. "Stubborn as usual."

He dropped the nosegay in my water glass. He gestured toward the chair. "May I?"

He sat down and crossed his long legs. I thought, not for the first time, that he looked like one of those elongated figures by El Greco. But he was tanned, not a ghostly white – the result of numerous trips to Puerto Rico. He kept an apartment there.

"Tell me what they've done to you." He nodded toward the IV stand. "Besides fill you with their lethal mixtures."

I told him, briefly, about the procedure, my voice still

hoarse. He seemed uncomfortable. It struck me for the first time that he might be one of those people made nervous by illness.

"I found a note from David Donnenfeld under my door last night. He said you've been making no end of trouble." He paused. "I got back just in time."

That was my cue, very welcome, to change the subject. "Where were you, Miles?"

"Idra. Or should I say Hydra? I think the latter. I've never climbed so many steps in my life. The whole place is one giant staircase."

I remembered the island. I had gone there once, in another life, when Tim Currier and I were living together.

"I was in Athens," he went on, "and I thought, why not visit Andrew Bullard? He has a house on that wretched island at the top, it turned out, of a stairway designed for Titans. You know, he writes those dreadful novels about the British Secret Service."

I nodded. Miles knew a lot of writers. He himself wrote gothic romances.

"He couldn't have been kinder. Not only did he give me an excellent lunch, entirely devoid of squid, but invited one of the locals in for some postprandial entertainment. It was marvelous. After he left, I told Andrew the young man had cost me a chapter."

"Thank you, Balzac."

"Oh dear, caught in another plagiarism."

I thought about Miles's chapters. He'd come to fiction late in life – a dozen years ago when he was still in his fifties, long after his dance career had ended. He had a knack for baroque plots – ancient curses, poison bracelets, sliding panels, the whole bit. A master of the marvelous. He had published a few, paperback originals mostly, but then the offers had dried up. His books didn't sell, or there were disputes with the editors – he never told me exactly – but I gathered he was no longer in demand. And yet he never stopped manufacturing plots. They dropped fully-formed into his mind at the oddest times.

I recalled an afternoon we had spent in Central Park, waiting to see a performance of *Titus Andronicus*. He had made up, quite easily and on the spot, a complicated story about an aged ballerina who had poisoned her various husbands, enslaved her handsome servant ("Looked just like Erick Hawkins in his prime, my dear, if you can remember back that far") and had built a theater in the wing of her estate in Somerset. There, each Saturday at midnight she danced the great roles of her youth – Giselle, Aurora, Odette/Odile – with her Slavic beauty of a houseboy as partner.

I had lain on the warm grass listening, no longer aware of the shouts of the baseball players, the soccer teams, the kids with their frisbees, as Miles spun out his absurd melodrama in a clipped, controlled voice. I was his captive. When he finally finished I sat up, hypnotized. Even Shakespeare's *Titus Andronicus*, coming up, would probably fascinate me less. I had to shake my head, like a dog coming out of water, to rid myself of his fantasies. "How on earth do you dream these things up?" I'd asked, but he had pooh-poohed my admiration and deprecated his talent. "I just let my unconscious take over," he'd said.

Now, looking at him in the hospital room, I couldn't help contrast his henna rinse, his plucked eyebrows, the light line of mascara circling his cloudy blue eyes, with his powers as a spinner of tales. There seemed to be a contradiction. Or was there? Maybe he represented some shamanistic power that dated back to the first tribes, that straddled the sexes, that derived its power from androgyny.

"Now tell me about your plans. When you get out of this morgue." He fluttered his eyelids.

I started in on my new medical schedule, but once again I had the impression he wasn't listening. Finally I asked, "Are you going to see David soon?"

It was Miles, after all, who had sent David Donnenfeld to the Longacre School. I had never quite fixed the nature of their early friendship, but they had kept in touch over the years.

"As a matter of fact, I expect him for dinner this evening. I called him after I read his note and invited him. The dear boy has brought me a gift from Mexico City."

"He brought me something too. Probably the same thing."

He lifted a hand. "Don't tell me."

I lifted my hand too, but the wrong hand and the wrong gesture. The IV fell out. My hand started to bleed. "Oh my God." I sank back.

"I'll get the nurse, shall I?"

I motioned to the signal pull, but he was gone.

After they stuck me again, Miles watching intently, I expected him to mutter some apology and leave. He hadn't seemed comfortable. But to my surprise he sat down again. "I thought you might like to hear a story," he said.

I glanced at him. His eyelids had flanged down, a new somnolence had come over him. He was going into his story-telling mode. I recalled the yarn he had spun as we waited to get into *Titus Andronicus*, and then another window opened and I remembered that when I was sick as a child, my mother would sometimes read me a story. We would merge, at least for the duration of the tale, and I would imagine that safety was possible between us.

In reflex, I closed my eyes too and settled back.

"I thought of it on the way here," he began. "The subway is so depressing, and there's that Cretan labyrinth at 59th Street. I suppose that's why my best ideas come to me underground – I don't dare absorb the surroundings. Of course, I'll go home and write it down, but maybe you'd like a preview." He paused. "If it bores you, you must stop me."

And so he started, in his precise, controlled voice, never hesitating, never groping for a phrase or a figure of speech. I thought perhaps Homer had relayed his epics with the same sureness – or Isak Dinesen. It was the mark of someone who understood that surfaces, artfully arranged, light up the depths most clearly.

"There's a man who lives, shall we say, in New Jersey, your home state. The town of Hasbrouck Heights, perhaps, a community of hardworking people who commute to New York, where they work in a variety of unglamorous trades. Our man, whose name is Bill Peppier, is in the printing business. He owns a small company, consisting of three multiliths, and specializes in leaflets, publicity brochures, quarterly reports, and so forth. But Bill is not your usual ink-stained pressman. He has a secret ambition. He wants to be a writer. Yes, a writer. These dreams started when he was young, when his father read *The Wind in the Willows* to him, or perhaps the tales of Andersen and Grimm. And so this urge, this itch to scribble, has stayed with Bill through youth and into middle age, diverting his attention from his business, from his wife and two children, from the community problems of Hasbrouck Heights. You see, he is a marked man, an artist."

Miles paused. I could sense him peering at me. Had I fallen asleep? I opened one eye. "American parents don't read *The Wind in the Willows* to their kids."

"Of course. How careless of me. What shall it be?"

"Dr. Seuss. The Oz books."

"Thank you. To proceed. Bill has ambitions, but great difficulty in carrying them out. He can't concoct a plot. He's good at dialogue, character, setting, but not the story line. He simply cannot think of interesting occurrences in sequence."

Another pause. I was quite interested now, the IV, the soreness in my hand, my raw throat, forgotten.

"And then someone moves into their neighborhood who precipitates a crisis. He is a single man, a spinster, of rather flamboyant aspect. His name is Stefan duPene, although everyone, the ladies especially, suspect that this is a made-up label, a *nom de plume*. It so happens that Stefan, unlike Bill, is a master of invention. He can plot a short story in an hour. He can dream up a novel in an afternoon. He is, in fact, an American version of Miss Barbara Cartland, but without the Jacobean manor and the ancient oak tree from which she plucks acorns to gild for important visitors. Not only can Stefan duPene fabricate these fictions, he can turn them into saleable books. He has an agent and a publisher. He is, in short, a mildly successful writer of ladies' romances."

I turned to glance at him. His eyes were still half-closed.

"To continue. One day Stefan knocks on the door of the Peppier home. His refrigerator is broken and he has been told that Bill, like so many American men, is good at engine repair. Bill, who is rather good-natured, agrees to run down the street and look at it. While there in Stefan's house, he discovers a cache of story ideas – hundreds of three-by-five cards, each with a dense, complicated plot waiting to be fleshed into prose narrative. Bill's heart starts beating fast. His palms turn icy. This is exactly what he needs. With these cards, these ideas, his dream of being a writer could become a reality. He would earn his father's posthumous esteem, the respect of his colleagues, his wife's love – to say nothing of getting his name in the Hasbrouck Heights *Herald*. Of course, he does not mention this to Stefan. But after repairing the fridge, he goes home in a state of utter confusion."

I heard a sharp, in-drawn breath. Miles was excited by his story. I was too. "What happened then?" I asked – the question, I realized, of millions of children at millions of bedtimes who understand that the world is not only explained by stories but that the stories themselves are the world.

"Well, let me see. It was about here that the subway train arrived and I had to get off." He shifted position. I watched his eyes come slowly into focus. He was back in the present. "There will be a theft of the story cards and perhaps a murder. Murders are so important in fiction. The American public seems to demand them. Proof that life in this country is really a blood sport."

"Who's going to get murdered?"

"Stefan, obviously. Bill Peppier, you see, has certain Mafia connections through his printing company – not that any of them can read very well – and he hires someone to steal the shoeboxes containing the three-by-five cards. But something goes wrong. Stefan smells a rat. There are complications. Perhaps drugs are involved – I'm not sure."

"Then the murder doesn't take place?"

He shivered and sat up. "I don't know. I probably won't find out until I take that wretched subway home. Do you want me to call you later and tell you how it comes out?"

I shook my head, laughing. "I can live without it."

"Of course you can." He stood up and came to the bed,

leaning over me. His eyes, in the late afternoon dimness, were dark blue – almost a midnight color. "You know you must get well and stay well, Bruce."

The force of his good will enveloped me. "I'll try, Miles."

"A great many people depend on you. You must pull yourself together."

I almost laughed at his simplistic recipe – but again the force of his kindness overwhelmed me. I recalled that, after sending David to us at the music school, Miles had paid all his lesson and tuition fees for several years. "I'll do what I can," I replied, lamely. "We'll see."

"Yes, we'll see." He stood up straight, his aplomb asserting itself. "You haven't tiddled your last wink, my dear, I'm quite sure."

He raised his hand in blessing, spun around and slithered out. Oddly, I felt optimistic for the first time in weeks. If there was any magic to be applied to my condition, Miles Halloran would supply it.

An hour later, a nurse woke me, asking if I wanted to use the pisspot.

§ § §

Angela Michaels came to take me home the next afternoon, Tuesday. She had removed her mouse tail and was wearing slacks. The best part was the lifting of the IV stick. I almost levitated out of bed and into my clothes. The humiliation, the invasion of privacy, was over for now. My customary self was waiting for me downstairs next to the Cashier's Office – a coat of many colors I couldn't wait to fling around my shoulders.

Clutching my overnight bag and my vial of Septra pills, I insisted that we walk the three blocks to Twelfth

Street. Angela put her arm through mine and kept up a steady stream of chatter as we walked. I stumbled once at the curb, and her grasp was like iron. The hint of a new, unwelcome dependency assailed me, but I put it out of my mind. When I reached home everything would be okay.

Once inside, I was filled with quiet joy. I looked around the living room – a dream-grotto filled with the mementoes of a life in music. Not only scores and records and tapes and piano but framed recital posters from school, publicity stills signed by our more illustrious graduates, a few relative rarities like a Rubenstein autograph and a Flagstad letter, both framed. This was the second skin of my superimposed identity. Not that it was all of me, not by a long shot, but it was a valued part, I started to express some of this to Angela, but she heard something in my tone she didn't like – self-pity maybe – and cut me off. Angela believed in staying in the present. She was right, of course. We switched the topic to groceries. She would go shopping for me.

When she came back, with a few additions of her own (a lethal mixture of tofu and sun-dried tomatoes, among other things), she had the afternoon *Post*, my least favorite tabloid, notoriously homophobic. The front headline was absurd and I resolved not to open it.

After putting away the groceries, Angela came into the living room. "I hope you're doing your visualizing, honey." I assured her I was.

"Do you want me to fix you something to eat?"

"No thanks."

She didn't want to leave but finally she did, with more warnings about proper diet. After she left, I found an old can of El Paso chili and heated it up. Full of deadly fats and chemicals, I thought, spooning it up ravenously.

Just what the doctor ordered. It was the perfect antidote to those beets and baked potatoes at St. Vincent's.

I don't know why I opened the *Post* after all. Maybe I was momentarily bored. Maybe there were vibrations in the room. Maybe the information was looking for me. At any rate, I turned the pages idly, noting the screaming heads, the lurid photos, the tawdriness of it all. And then my eye landed and I knew that it was for me.

WEST SIDE WRITER FOUND MURDERED

Death of Mystery-Romance Author
Resembles One of His Own Plots

I read quickly. Miles Halloran – but why had I known it was Miles before I saw his name? – had been discovered by a neighbor this morning, in his apartment on 81st Street. The neighbor, Mrs. Alberta Jaeckel, had noticed the front door ajar. There were no signs of forced entry and a preliminary search of the premises revealed nothing missing. Halloran had been listening to a music tape at the time of his death. His body had been badly hacked by a large blade. Death had been due to loss of blood. An investigation was being handled at the 20th Precinct. There were certain questions about the victim's lifestyle.

I read the story three times, numbly. I had seen Miles only yesterday afternoon in the hospital. He had passed on his blessing, a wish for my recovery, and now he himself was gone, another witness to the fragility of things. I stood up and started pacing around the apartment, touching certain objects as if they were talismans and could save me, or save Miles. It wasn't my first brush with murder in New York, not after all these years, but it cut the closest. Who could replace Miles in my life? Who could supply that rare blend of cynicism and magic? Even though our paths crossed only occasionally, we were always aware of the other's presence. The tie went deep – I couldn't begin to explain why – and now it had been severed.

The next minute I thought of David. Hadn't Miles said he was due for dinner last night? I was just starting toward the phone when it rang.

"Bruce?" The voice was low, rushed, the familiar calm gone.

"David."

"You heard?"

"Just now, in the *Post*."

"My God, that reporter must have walked in with the cops. Mrs. Jaeckel called me right after she called the police."

"Who's she?"

"She lives across the hall. I've known her for years, through Miles. I gave one of her kids lessons for a while."

"Do they have any idea ...?"

The reply was fainter. "Miles knew hundreds of people. They're going through his address book. They might even call you."

"Do they have any leads?"

There was a pause, the pain humming along the wire. "I was at his place last night. He fixed dinner. I ... I left the program from Mexico City there. You know how he likes to know what I play. The cops saw it right off. They called me at noon today."

I was too surprised to respond for a moment. "They don't think you had something to do with ...?"

"I don't know what they think. But they know I was on the premises last night. I ... I think I should have a lawyer."

My mind went into overdrive. I reviewed some contacts and promised to supply a name within the hour. Then another thought hit me. "Maybe you should come over here and spend the night, David. Maybe you shouldn't be alone."

He vetoed that idea, said he'd be okay, and the next minute he was sobbing into the phone. Miles and David – it was a connection, a relationship – that went back to David's first explorations of the world of professional music. His loss was much greater than mine. Miles, in ways unknown to me, had seen him through the first growing-up time.

I listened to him weep, urging him to let it all out, until he came to the end of it. Again he refused to come over and spend the night. But after I hung up, I found the apartment, my safe place, filled with images of death again.

3

"Can you get AIDS from kissing?"

"Can you get AIDS from mosquitoes?"

"I had sex with a Navajo Indian, he never heard of AIDS and he wouldn't use a condom, what are my chances?"

"I'm in a mental institution. They locked me up on account of they think I have AIDS. Can you get me out?"

"What does heterosexual mean?"

The calls buzzed from the headset into my ear, my phone light flashing the instant I hung up. I could feel the fear, the craziness, out there. I looked at my watch. Just three o'clock. I'd been here since one, my Saturday afternoon stint on the AIDS Hotline. Another two hours to go. I'd volunteered for once-a-week duty almost a year ago, inspired by the example of Shirley Scott, one of our graduates, and a soprano who didn't concentrate solely on her career. She'd brought me here to the Hotline offices in a decrepit office building near Union Square, sweet-talked me into a weekend of training. Now I was an expert, more or less.

I looked around the operators' area. Shirley was

punching up her terminal, locating a test site for a caller. I could hear her rich, beautifully modulated voice advise that there was no public health facility for free HIV testing in Dothan, Alabama.

I hadn't been listening to my own call. "No sir," I said at last, "finger-fucking a prostitute won't infect you, even if you have a hang nail."

"No ma'am, Laconia, Arkansas is not a high-risk area."

"No, Ginny, I can't write your school assignment for you, why don't you ask your librarian to help?"

"Well, Senator Helms is wrong about swimming pools."

I punched my deactivator code and removed my headset. Time for a cup of coffee. We were allowed a fifteen minute break midway through our four hours. I touched Shirley's shoulder on the way out, pointing to the volunteer lounge. Her slim brown hand closed over mine but she shook her head. I wondered what her interlocutors would say if they were told Operator 238 was singing four Susannas, three Rosinas and one Zerbinetta at the Met this season, two of them to be broadcast.

There was nobody in the lounge and I poured myself some of the dark, bitter fluid dripped by Mr. Coffee. Then I checked the cooler. Some cheese-and-cracker packets and two cups of ancient yogurt.

It had been almost a week since my discharge from St. Vincent's, since Miles's murder, since David's first interrogations by the police. I had found him an attorney, who had sat in on the questioning, but the police had made no allegations, no threats. David admitted he had been on the premises the night of the murder. Yes, those were his fingerprints on the Callas tape which had been inserted in the cassette player, because he had brought it as a gift and wanted to play it for Miles. Yes, he and

Miles had been good friends for almost ten years. He had left the premises about eleven p.m., when Miles was very much alive. His first knowledge of the crime had been when Miles's neighbor called him at noon the next day. There had been nothing odd or suspicious in Miles's behavior that night. He had just returned from a trip to Greece and appeared to be in good spirits.

David had told me all this at dinner several nights after the murder. "They wanted to know the exact nature of my relationship to Miles," he told me at one point, "and I got sore. I said, 'If you want to know if I went to bed with him, that's none of your fucking business.'"

He also said the police had asked for confirmation, an eye witness to prove that he had actually left at eleven, when Miles was still alive. "But how?" he asked me. "I took a cab home. I didn't see anyone I knew. Why would I, at that hour?"

I had tried to offer reassurances. "They're just trying to intimidate you. You had absolutely no motive for killing Miles. Just the opposite, in fact – one of his oldest friends. They're just fishing. You've probably heard the last of them."

"I hope so," he groused. He hadn't been able to practice since Miles's death – something had changed between him and his music. When he said this he had the slightly panicked look I had seen on other musicians' faces when they learned they had nodes on their vocal cords or rheumatoid arthritis in their fingers. "I think I'm going to have to cancel the Canada tour," he added. "I mean, if I can't practice, I can't go."

I advised patience, no irrevocable cancellations. Something might break in the case very soon.

"The reason I don't feel like practicing isn't because the police are asking me questions, Bruce. It's because

Miles was hacked into little pieces. How can you make beautiful sounds in a world like that? It becomes ... well, totally irrelevant. Arabesques on somebody's grave. I mean, what's the point?"

I didn't argue. David would have to come to terms with violent death in his own way, in his own time. I suspected that music would be the catalyst for that process, but there was no use arguing the point now.

"*Ay bendito*, what's this about you being in the hospital?"

I was yanked out of my reverie by Reginaldo, one of the staff supervisors. He pulled me off the saggy couch and gave me a monumental *abrazo*. Reginaldo was tall, bespectacled, overweight. His family had moved from Ponce to New York when he was four. He'd grown up in the barrio.

"Yeah, Reginaldo, last week. Just for a bronchoscopy."

He wanted to know everything. I told him about my slight case of pneumocystis – a walking case – and how the Septra was working. I still suffered from fatigue but I had developed a new talent – I could cat-nap anywhere.

"Okay, who's your doctor?" When I told him he replied, "Zinsser is good, but if you ever need a second opinion I want you to see Barbara Holthaus. She's a wonder woman, she'll keep you alive forever."

He wrote down a name and address. Typical, I thought, the most useful help possible.

"We're having operator appreciation night at the Pasha next week, did you get your invitation? Are you coming?"

Reginaldo continued with the menu of delights we could expect at the disco – drinks, buffet, dancing, all free. "I want you to bring someone hunky who'll go home with you afterward for safe sex."

"Who're you bringing?"

He shook his head. "It's my vacation. I'll be in Puerto Rico. I want to see my cousin Lito. He's doing a one-man show at the Tapio. He writes his own monologues, like Jacopo Morales."

"How do you get to be a famous actor in Puerto Rico?"

"The newspapers, *pupi. El Vocero. Nuevo Día. El Reportero.* And there's television, also, *The Star.* That," he concluded, "prints reviews in English for the ignorant ones."

I grinned. I knew *The Star.* When I visited Miles in Puerto Rico I read it every morning. "I even met the drama critic for *The Star,*" I said. "At a party. I forget his name."

"Sonny Barowski."

"That's it."

"He lives on Calle Cristo, right by the Capilla. The most beautiful apartment in Old San Juan." Reginaldo kissed his fingertips. "Lito took me there once. You can see the harbor. Catano. Isla Grande. La Fortaleza. Everything."

My mind started whirling. "Would your cousin – what's his name, Lito?"

"Miguel Luces Echeverria." The melodious syllables echoed around the room. "Lito is short for Miguelito."

"Do you think he'd pass a message to Sonny Barowski?"

"Is it important?"

The party at Miles's apartment took shape in my mind. I had been introduced to Barowski, a man around sixty with a fierce, defeated look and a pronounced limp. I had recognized a familiar type – the Caribbean castaway. Too many wives, too much booze, too many disappointments. But he was a good critic, steeped in the Spanish and English classics. He had told me, in a drunken confidence that evening, that Miles had done him a great favor once. "Yes, it's important. Tell him his friend Miles Halloran was murdered."

"Who?"

I spelled it out, gave a few details. I also scribbled my phone number for him to pass on to Barowksi.

"*Ay bendito*," he said when I finished, "if it isn't AIDS, it's murder."

"Have you ever thought of moving back to PR, Reginaldo?"

He shook his head. "There is where I live. This is where we struggle." He smiled. "Besides, I got a rent-stabilized apartment on Perry Street."

I thought briefly of Socrates. He had been offered the chance to escape Athens and the death sentence but had refused. He would stay with his city to the bitter end.

Reginaldo looked at me. "I won't be at the Pasha, so I'm giving the operators some appreciation right now. He gave me a second hug, more powerful than the first.

For some reason, I didn't feel sleepy any more. Reginaldo had refreshed me. Besides, my break was over. It was time to go back to America's nightmares.

It was my luck to get Sandra, our resident kook, on the first call after my break. She recognized my voice right away. "Is that you, one-oh-four, where you been?"

I let Sandra go on about her mother, the men who took advantage of her, her desire to meet me in person. It was strictly against orders to let a crank caller take up phone time, but my mind was elsewhere. I shook my head, Sandra's words tickling my ear like demented gnats. "I bet we could have some fun, why won't you come and visit me? Why won't you tell me your name?"

It was clear why Sandra found men so predatory – she was determined to be a victim.

"I have to sign off, Sandra, lotta calls waiting."

"Why won't you talk to me?" Her voice rose to a whine.

"I'm sorry, that's all for today."

A gentle click and I was free. I waited a moment then punched the access button. This female caller, who said she was a grandmother, wanted to know about anal sex. Twenty years ago you couldn't mention the subject in polite society.

Rubber up, America!

§ § §

On Monday morning at 11 o'clock, a busy hour, Erica came into my office.

She closed the door behind her. "Bruce, there are two detectives here." She coughed – her usual sign of tension. "They asked if you could spare a few minutes."

Erica's face, usually so composed, was alive with curiosity. "It's about Miles Halloran," I said, "you remember him. He used to come to our evening recitals." She didn't. "He was murdered exactly a week ago." I didn't mention David's connection. "Ask them to come in."

They exuded size. Maybe it was their manner or the bulges under their jacket or their generally unapologetic air. They showed me ID, then shook hands.

Lieutenant Kerrison, Lieutenant Meyer, both from Homicide, 20th Precinct.

Kerrison seemed to be in charge.

"Dr. Pittman, we understand that you were a close friend of Mr. Halloran." I nodded and he went on. "If you don't mind, sir, we'd like to ask a few questions."

I sat back. "I'll be glad to help."

They asked first how we met. Meyer took out a flip-top notebook and balanced it on his knee. I told them I had met Miles on the beach in Puerto Rico on my first visit there about fifteen years ago. We had struck up a conversation. One thing had led to another, and he had invited us to his apartment for drinks.

"Us?" asked Meyer, writing.

"I was vacationing with a friend."

He nodded and wrote that down.

"Mr. Halloran traveled a lot, judging from his passport. Was there any particular reason for that?"

I told him that Miles was restless, a writer, always looking for new backgrounds.

"What kind of books did Mr. Halloran write?"

That was easy. I described his flair for gothic plots.

"He make enough from these books to keep an apartment in New York and Puerto Rico both?"

"I'm not really sure. He used to complain about money but not in recent years. Maybe he inherited something. He came from a well-to-do family in England."

"Was Mr. Halloran a user of illegal substances?"

"Definitely not. He was very fussy about his health."

"Was Mr. Halloran in the habit of bringing strangers home late at night?"

That was easy too. Miles rarely took chances, not with bar acquaintances, with hustler services or street types.

"One last question, sir. Do you know of anyone who might have wanted to kill him?"

I shook my head. "Miles had dozens of friends. He was charming and popular. I can't imagine anyone who would do this."

The notebook was closed. They stood up. Kerrison, the taller of the two, had a few freckles spattered on his face. He had probably been covered with them as a child. I had a sudden glimpse of his history – a school called Holy Name, nights at Fordham or Seton Hall where he played basketball and hockey, a big wedding, and a wife who worried about his safety. His father might have traveled the same route before him ...

"I understand you've seen my friend David Donnenfeld," I said as they were getting ready to leave.

Kerrison turned.

"I just wanted to say there's no way David could be linked to this. He and Miles were close friends. Had been for years. In fact, Miles was sort of his patron. He paid his tuition at this school for the first few years."

Something crossed Kerrison's face and I realized I had said too much. Had I actually provided a new connection? I stammered something about too much crime, too many psychopaths on the streets. They thanked me and departed, first asking me to get in touch if I heard anything new.

I sat at my desk for a long time, trying to control myself. At last Erica tiptoed in and I gave her some details of the situation. Watching her reaction, her obvious fascination with the crime, it occurred to me that Miles's murder, except for those who knew him, now belonged to every tabloid reader, to every TV addict. The loss of a life was more than offset by the gain in sensation. Even Erica, who was 35 years old and sensible in every way, had been swept away by the lurid possibilities. Suddenly I recalled something Miles had said that last afternoon in the hospital. *The American public demands murders; they're proof that life in this country is a blood sport.*

His words had made no impression on me at the time. I had been as desensitized as everyone else.

And then Erica reminded me that the Longacre

Quartet, our newest project, was upstairs waiting for me to sit in on their rehearsal. They were working on the last Beethoven quartet, God help us. I made my way upstairs, hoping against hope I'd be able to concentrate on the music.

4

"THIS JAMBALAYA COMES FROM one of my grand-mother's recipes. It has okra in it. I hope it's not too spicy for you, Bruce."

Clay Lemaitre, our host for the evening, was being Southern and gracious. I made some obligatory sounds. The concoction I was forking struck me as suitable for someone on half rations in a Turkish prison.

"Oh, it's delicious, Clay," David, sitting across from me, put in. His remark was possibly sincere and he wanted everyone to be happy.

"More wine, Bruce?" Clay lifted the bottle of Pouilly-Fuissé. One glass was my limit these days but I held up my glass anyway. I didn't get this stuff every night, bottled sunlight.

We were at a table by the window, Central Park spread below us like a giant postage stamp. I had to admit that, aside from the jambalaya of antique provenance, the evening had been pleasant. Clay was a good host and his apartment was made for entertaining. Deep chintz-covered chairs, richly textured rugs, handsome brass lamps, cut crystal that glinted in blues and reds.

And of course, books everywhere – lavish, expensive books, overflowing the waist-high bookcases, the tables, the side chairs. Clay was head of a medium-size publishing house, Lightning Books. He and David had met in a Village bar about ten months ago. I still wasn't sure where – or how far – their relationship was going. But it was obviously serving some good purpose. Now, more than two weeks after Miles's murder, David was back at the piano, talking about his Canada tour again. I liked to think that my few, well-selected words had eased him over the rough places, but tonight, in this lush apartment on Central Park West, I realized I had probably contributed less than Clay.

I examined Clay again, noting the shaggy graying hair, the strong nose and jaw, the massive shoulders and sensual mouth. He had told us an amusing story tonight over drinks. Once, when he was a kid in New Orleans, he had been sitting in church when he heard the tinkle of an ice-cream cart outside. He had whispered to his father that he wanted a cone *now*. Together they had slipped out of the service. "Whatever I wanted, my Daddy gave me," he informed us, "I never had to ask him twice." It was undoubtedly the key to his personality, I thought somewhat sourly, but Clay seemed highly pleased. I figured he had gone through life without having to ask for many things twice, including David.

"Clay tells me your tour went well, David." Rita Osterkamp, the fourth member of our party, hadn't spoken much. She worked with Clay at Lightning Books, his second-in-command. She was tall, slender, with dark hair and olive-tinted skin, heading into the shoals of middle age with a pleasant, self-effacing manner. I had liked her right off.

"Pretty well." David frowned. "I don't know about

those Latino audiences. They make an awful lot of noise, worse than the Italians."

"I went to a Marta Argerich concert in Caracas a few years ago," Rita went on, glancing at Clay. "I was down there seeing Jorge Jiménez, we were trying to get the translation rights. I thought the audience was quite well-behaved."

"They pay attention to her," David replied. "She's one of them."

As the small talk went on, my sense of well-being increased. The events of the past few weeks, worries about my health, seemed remote here. I was safe in this penthouse, this cloud-capped circle of friendship and good will.

Half an hour later we were back in the living area, coffee cups in hand.

The conversation came around to Miles. By mutual consent we had avoided it during the meal.

David started. "The police asked me not to leave the country, did I tell you that, Bruce?"

I shook my head. "I thought they were finished with you."

"For now. But they want me around just in case."

Clay cut in. "Jim Slade has given us an opinion on that. David can go to Canada if he wants. He will have to furnish an itinerary to the authorities and stick to it, that's all."

Jim Slade, I knew, was the high-powered attorney Clay had brought in, to take the place of my own nomination.

"Also, be prepared to cancel a concert at short notice if they want me back here," David put in. He shook his head. "I'm still not absolutely sure I want to go."

"There's no reason you can't tour," Clay spoke authoritatively. We all watched David. His fingers were splayed on his thighs, tapping out unheard melodies.

"I don't see why they can't let him off the hook," I said. "They're just playing games with him."

"Of course they are," Clay rumbled. "That's what they do. It's a form of psychological warfare."

I started to protest that David was innocent but checked myself. Everybody knew that.

"I hadn't come across Miles Halloran in some years," Rita remarked in her mild way. "Was he working on anything at ... the time?"

"Miles never stopped dreaming up stories," I said, "it was as natural as breathing."

"And he didn't even start till he was in his fifties," David added. "He told me he was walking around Granada one afternoon, the gardens of the Generalife, I think, when a story about the Moors and the ghost of Washington Irving popped into his head." He laughed. "The funniest part was that he'd never read a word of Washington Irving."

"That must have been *The Gardens of Paradise*, Rita said. "That was the first Halloran title we published."

I looked at her. "That's an odd coincidence. I didn't know Lightning Books published Miles."

"We did for a short while," Clay interrupted. "Then we parted ways."

"Oh?" I floated the syllable like a question mark, but Clay's lips were closed.

"It just didn't work out," Rita said, with a glance at Clay.

"He never really learned to write saleable fiction," Clay said briskly, closing the subject. He got up. "I've got something to show you."

He went into the bedroom and a moment later

appeared with a video cassette. "It's the Bolshoi doing *L'Age d'Or*," he said.

Without waiting for approval he wheeled the TV forward and slipped the cassette into the VCR. We settled back. The ballet was highly athletic and took place on a murkily-lit stage. However, the Russian male in the lead role was magnificent. Nothing effetely western about him. He might have left a Siberian coal mine for a few minutes. We watched without speaking.

When the tape finished, Rita spoke. "Well," she said, in a tone that might have been interpreted in a dozen ways. Whether she was thrilled intellectually or physically I couldn't tell.

"That's Miles's tape," David put in. "I borrowed it from him a few months ago." He seemed to sag. "I guess we can keep it now." He turned toward Rita. "That reminds me, I brought that mask for you. The one from Miles's shipment."

"We keep coming back to Miles," I said, trying not to sound accusatory. My euphoria of the dinner table was evaporating. Fatigue was hovering over me. "What mask is that?"

David said that Miles had been bringing plaster masks and other tourist stuff from Puerto Rico to New York. "He was doing it as a favor to a friend on the island. He passed them on to some wholesaler in the Bronx, also to some tourist shops around town. I guess he made a little money out of it."

"I hoped you picked out a nice one for me," Rita said.

"They're all the same. They're used in one of the religious fiestas down there, sort of a blend of African animism and Catholicism. Sometimes Miles painted the masks, gave the eyes shadows and made the cheeks pink and did curlicue mustaches, stuff like that. Remember how small his apartment was? Well, he got a double ship-ment a few weeks ago and asked me to store some boxes for him. I still have them."

He went to the vestibule and came back with a bag. From it he extracted a white plaster mask. It was quite uninteresting – smooth features, large eyeholes, mouth like a gash. "They must have an assembly line down there," he said, "though they're carelessly packed. Lots of them seem to be broken."

"Well, I'll decorate it myself," Rita said. She took the mask and bag from David. "This working person has to get home," she said. "Do you want to share a cab, Bruce?"

I did. I would drop her in Chelsea, then proceed on to 12th Street.

We were collected at the door, Rita and I ready to leave, when Clay said, "I thought Miles looked poorly after he came back from Greece."

I tried to recollect how he'd looked when he visited me in the hospital, but the details were blurry. I was seeing him through a haze of drugs. "Maybe he did, Clay. Maybe he had something serious on his mind. But we'll never know."

Our goodnights were a little strained. There was something about David's staying behind that triggered an old, useless proprietorship in me. And the talk of Miles had made us all uncomfortable.

I was glad of Rita's company going downtown. She filled me in on Clay's background. His people were prom-inent politically in Louisiana – judges, a state senator, a newspaper owner. He had two married sisters there. Even though he had exiled himself from all that, a residue remained. I agreed – he transmitted power and status without trying. Rita had worked for him for almost ten years, since he started Lightning Books.

Before getting out at 18th Street, she pressed her business card into my hand, also some money for the fare. "Just in case you need something, Bruce, please call. We're practically neighbors." She brushed her cheek against mine, leaving me touched and surprised.

I tried not to think of David and Clay as I got ready for bed. It was truly none of my business – an empty claim. David had had many affairs over the years, as necessary to his music as scales and arpeggios, but this one bothered me. What was the attraction? Even though Clay was a cultivated man, there was something coarse underneath. Was that the lure – opposites? But David, I knew, despite his delicacy, his magical connection to his music, had something hard and immovable at his core. He was no weak reed looking for someone to give him shape.

I gave up at last. Whatever the dynamic between them, the transfer of power or need, it couldn't be reduced to some simple syntax. I chuckled to myself. Maybe it was good sex and nothing more.

Who could have analyzed my life with Hector, when I was in my late twenties, David's age now? From the outside we must have looked like a total mismatch. Hector from Santo Domingo, his father a professional breeder of fighting cocks, his mother barely literate. Setting up house together was absurd on the face of it – a *mesalliance* that couldn't last a month. But the outsider wouldn't have known about our nights holding each other, or the confusion we were able to share, or the hostility of the world we were able to fend off together. None of that information was available to the casual inspector. And the same must be true of David and Clay. It was impertinent of me even to speculate. Certainly David's playing, at least until the last few weeks, had reflected the fact that something new was happening in his life.

Time to drop the subject. I slipped the Callas tape into my bedside cassette and listened to it again. When she started on the *Regnava nel silenzio*, my attention wandered and I thought about weight. Why had she gone on that diet? She never sang like this after 1955, which meant she'd had only a half-dozen great years. And she had died in Paris, immured in her apartment, refusing to see her friends, her identity shattered. Take her voice away and she was nothing – or so she thought.

And then, quite clearly, I heard Clay's rumbly voice in my ear and a jolt went through me. "I thought Miles looked poorly after he came back from Greece." The words echoed. There was something wrong. Miles had been killed just twenty-four hours after his return. I could almost reconstruct his last day.

He had arrived late at night, Sunday, September 14, to find a note from David under his door, notifying him that I would be in St. Vincent's the following day. The next afternoon, Monday, a little after four, he had paid me a visit. That night David had come for dinner, bringing the Callas tape and departing around eleven. Miles had been murdered later that same evening. I had read about it the next day, Tuesday, in the *Post*, after my discharge from the hospital. *When could Clay have seen him?*

I went over the schedule again, looking for cracks and seams. Was it possible they had met for lunch? Miles had complained about the subway trip downtown from his apartment. And Clay's days were undoubtedly busy. A lunch date seemed unlikely. Had they met after Miles left the hospital – in the late afternoon? But Miles had said he'd find the end of his story on the subway trip home, and offered to phone me with the details. And David had been due for dinner, so there must have been some kitchen chores to be done. I turned everything over in my mind some more. Was it possible that Clay had paid Miles a visit after David left?

I twisted and turned for a while, sleep impossible despite my fatigue. I switched on the lamp and dialed David's number. His machine – of course. He was spending the night at Clay's. I left a message and hung up, more fretful than ever. A few minutes later the phone rang. I reached for it quickly.

"Hello, is this Bruce Pittman?"

The voice was echoey, as if coming from inside a rain barrel. I didn't recognize it.

"This is Sonny Barowski. In Puerto Rico."

"Sonny! We have a rotten connection. I can hardly hear you."

He let out a snarl of laughter. "All the connections in Puerto Rico are rotten. We have to yell."

I thought of all those phone lines undersea being nibbled by fish. "Okay," I yelled, "how are you?"

"I was disturbed to hear about Miles. Lito Echeverria told me an hour ago. Did they find out who did it?"

"They're still looking."

"I think they should look down here."

"Why?"

"Miles had some funny friends on the island. He was investigated by the Nick."

"By the who?"

"Negociado de Investigaciones Criminales. N-I-C. We call it the Nick."

"What for?"

"He was on the premises of a certain club when they made a raid. The club is known for being mixed up in drugs and prostitution."

"What was Miles doing there?"

"He claimed he was selling them one of his paintings,

and they let him go. But everybody smelled a rat."

I thought about the two detectives on the Halloran case. They might enjoy a trip to Puerto Rico but they'd never get authorization for it. "I don't know what I can do up here, Sonny," I replied, "the police like to do it their own way."

"Well," Sonny's voice was growing fainter, "if they want some leads, tell them to get in touch with me. It's something I'd like to do for Miles."

We chatted a bit more then signed off. I doused the light. The news that Miles had some sleazy friends on the island didn't really surprise me. I had met a few of them in his various apartments there – one-legged lottery vendors, drug dealers from the British Virgins, a "professor" who furnished under-age prostitutes to tourists, the flotsam and jetsam that washed up at the edge of two cultures. Not that Miles used, or abused, these services. They simply reflected his taste for the macabre, the same taste that led him to concoct gothic romances. They stimulated his imagination. And of course, he was always protected by his Britishness, that impregnable armor of respectability. He could go anywhere, do anything, and remain one of Queen Victoria's own.

I smiled into the darkness. I recalled a story he had told me last year, on his return from Istanbul. He had stayed in a cheap hotel overlooking the Bosphorus. One afternoon, he had emerged from his room to find men sitting in chairs and benches along the corridor. It seemed that each week a prostitute took a room on this particular floor in order to ply her trade. Miles had stood watching, fascinated. After each man left, the woman appeared in the door of her room and beckoned to the next in line. But as Miles stood there, one of the young men reached over and patted him lightly on the fanny. Then he had nodded in the direction of Miles's room.

"Of course you took him up on it," I said laughing.

Miles had batted his eyes fiercely. "Are you mad? Do you think I wanted that whore's knife between my ribs?"

Yes – a taste for sleaze and an even greater instinct for self-preservation. What miscalculation had led to his death?

David returned my call early next morning, before I left for school. I had a dozen questions on my lips, unwelcome questions about his relationship with Clay, but I suppressed them. There was only one question I had the right to ask. "Clay made a remark last night, David. It's been on my mind."

"Oh?"

"He said he thought Miles looked tired – I think he said poorly – after he came back from Greece. I've been doing some figuring and I don't see how Clay had time to see Miles. He was killed just twenty-four hours after he got home."

I sensed, rather than heard, a shift at the other end. I went on. "I was going to ask Clay, but I decided to ask you first."

At last he cleared his throat and spoke. "Clay came by Miles's apartment to pick me up after dinner. He'd been at some publishing shindig. You know, he lives just a few blocks away."

"You didn't tell me that."

"I thought it would complicate things."

"You didn't tell the police either."

"I didn't want to involve Clay."

My mind was working fast. "So you lied to the police. Or omitted essential information. If they find out, it puts you both in a bad position."

I heard a sigh at the other end. "We figured Miles's

sexual habits would be plastered all over the tabloids. You know how they are. If Clay was mixed up in that ... Well, he's pretty closeted at work."

I started to express skepticism about anyone's closet status in this day and age but David interrupted me. "I think the police know somebody else was there that night. That's why they keep after me. Why they don't want me to leave the country."

"How do they know?"

"There was a Schimmelpenninck butt mixed in with the dirty dinner dishes in the sink. Their forensic people told them Miles was a non-smoker. I would have claimed I'd smoked it but they trapped me. They got me to admit I didn't smoke before they told me about it."

I let that sink in. "I don't understand why you won't tell the truth, David. A friend comes by for a nightcap, you leave together, what's the big cover-up?"

"I told you, I don't like to involve Clay."

"But he's already involved. And now you have a perfect alibi, a witness who saw you leave when Miles was still alive."

A pause at the other end. "I guess you're right, Bruce, I should tell them."

"Today."

"Yeah."

But there was something still stopping him. I had a sudden flash on the possibility that David might compromise his career to save Clay.

I repeated my exhortations but his response was even weaker. I didn't have all the facts and, until I did, David would stay with his sacrifice. Clay was probably pressuring him.

After hanging up, I got ready to leave the house. The morning, early October, was blue and gold. As I turned the corner of Hudson, I could see the kids in the playground at Abingdon Square, scuffing a soccer ball. It was a day when, a few months ago, my spirits would have soared. No longer.

And then, as I turned down Charles Street and the school came into view, I had a sudden glimpse of my responsibilities in this. *David mustn't wreck his career out of some misplaced loyalty.* If he wouldn't help himself, then I'd have to help him. It was as simple as that.

I entered the school vestibule, hearing the customary wake-up sounds – students vocalizing, violins tuning, pianos banging, a few latecomers racing for class. This moment had always given me the most intense pleasure – Luddie and I had created all this out of nothing – and for a moment it did again. I saw quite clearly that even though David was not my lover – had never been, would never be – the link that connected us went even deeper than that. It derived from an ancient, unbreakable lineage. It went back to Beethoven's pupil Czerny and *his* pupil Liszt. From that circle of students onward to Anton Rubenstein and Paderewski, to Hoffman and Josef Lhévinne and to Rosina Lhévinne, his widow, who had been my teacher. This was my genealogical tree, and David's was the latest name on it. He was my charge, and as long as I believed in music and in the power of our peculiar art, I would have to make every effort to save him. It was my last obligation.

And then the day, with its delicious complications, began. I didn't give out until almost three, when a touch of fever sent me home.

5

DID YOU SEE THIS, BRUCE?"

Luddie Chametsky, my partner, was standing at my desk, waving a newspaper clipping.

"No, I didn't."

"Shirley Scott got a rave last night." He looked at me sympathetically. "You were really too sick to make it?"

I nodded, feeling awful. "I couldn't have made it to Avery Fisher last night if Toscanini had come back to lead the Philharmonic."

Luddie shook his head nervously. My health status confused and upset him. We had started this school together, and I suspected he had doubts about this ability to carry on alone. It was a subject we avoided – all but one aspect of it. I had informed him he would inherit my share.

"Well, she sang like an angel. Strauss should have been alive to hear it. Anne and I were both in tears."

I sat back, looking at Luddie. He was a hairy man. The hair swirled upward from his throat, arms, wrists, though he was going bald on top. A hair symphony. Maybe his wife loved him for that pelt – too much testosterone – but I couldn't help wondering how she felt about it in hot weather. Luddie had been Shirley's first teacher here, and still followed her career passionately.

"Was David there?" I asked. A rhetorical question. David wouldn't have missed Shirley doing the *Four Last Songs* with the Philharmonic for anything.

"As a matter of fact, he wasn't."

"He wasn't?"

"I figured he was touring. I don't keep up with him these days."

"No, he's ..." I choked off the sentence. No use going into all that. I hadn't talked to David for a week, not since our conversation the morning after Clay's dinner party. My demand that he notify the police of Clay's visit to Miles's apartment had obviously alienated him. And now he'd missed Shirley's debut with the Philharmonic. "Did Shirley say anything?"

Luddie chewed his lower lip. "We went to the Russian Tea Room afterward but nobody mentioned David. It was Shirley's night."

I looked down at my desk, covered with a pile of checks to be co-signed. I hadn't been here for a few days. "Well, he'll probably see the review and call her."

"If he misses it, there it is. Feast your eyes."

He dropped the *Times* review and walked off. From the rear Luddie was impressive in a different way. He had important buttocks – square and massive. It was hard to contradict a man with a rear like that, which his students discovered sooner or later.

I read the review, then turned my thoughts to David again. What had kept him from the concert?

Erica, dressed in a white, Grecian-type sheath, appeared in the doorway. "There's a Miss Osterkamp on the line."

I sensed a connection closing. Maybe Rita would know something about David. I nodded. Erica turned, leaving a vapor trail of Obsession behind her. It was Friday; I figured she had a date right after work.

Rita's warm voice caressed my ear. After inquiring about my health, she asked if we might have lunch. She'd be at her printer's on Varick in a few hours, reading the proof for their new catalog. Would I by any chance ...?

I was still a little shaky but I agreed. It might give me a boost. We arranged to meet at Tommaso's, one of the last joints in Little Italy where you could still get veal marsala for a decent price.

I was saved from further rumination by the appearance of Fiona McCleary. "Dr. Pittman."

I stood up. I always stood in her presence – some atavistic reaction, respect for the goddess.

"I am sorry to complain but circumstances force me."

She was wearing a cape today. Her grey hair was done up in sausage rolls. "I am not pleased with the tuning of the pianos in 307 and 309. But that is not my chief complaint. I feel that my advanced students are under-represented in next week's concert."

I observed Fiona's large face go through the contortions of blame, self-pity, outrage. It was a shame she was such a good teacher. Word-of-mouth about Miss McCleary had brought us dozens of students and kept them. She was indispensable and knew it.

"I must insist that at least three students be added to the recital list."

"I can add just one." I held up a finger. "I'd suggest Jane Sung."

"I'm sorry, that won't do at all."

As we bickered, both of us performing like veterans, I thought about David's first verdict on Fiona. "Too big," he'd said and refused to elaborate. Later I had discovered that she reminded him of a seventh-grade teacher who had humiliated him regularly.

At last we had it settled. Jane Sung and Diana Smalley would each play something brief. "I must say," she turned and bent her cloudy grey eyes on me, "I have missed you recently. No one else will really …" she cast around for the word, "… engage me."

She sailed out. I tried not to feel flattered. *May you be blessed with worthy adversaries.* Was that an old Chinese proverb or had I just made it up?

§ § §

Rita was at the bar, sipping a Cinzano. She was even taller now, thanks to heels. We moved to a table, where I ordered a Perrier. We looked at each other with something like affection and I marveled for the hundredth time at the chemistry between certain strangers. Could it be another result of reincarnation, like musical giftedness? Had Rita and I been close friends in a previous life? I decided to keep the question to myself. No use alarming her.

"How's Clay?" I asked after we had ordered.

"Clay is very busy. We all are. We're having a big do at the Harvard Club next week. Maybe you'd like to come."

It seems Lightning Books was starting a new line of romance novels – not the kind you read, the kind you watch. They were launching a set of video-novels under the overall title, *Shadows of Desire.*

"Oh my God," I said, closing my eyes

"Now don't condemn us in advance. We've got some of the best writers in the field – Kathleen Drake and Glinda Collins and Rosemary Renfrew. We've had a top-notch production house doing the casting and shooting. Frankly, we expect to make a bundle."

"Was this Clay's idea?"

She nodded. "He got us into audio – novels on tape – and now this. We've gone way over our heads to finance it." She gave a nervous smile. "Anyway, maybe you'd like to come next week. It's a press reception. It might be fun. I've got an extra invitation right here."

The evening at Clay's didn't come up until we were well into our entrées.

I debated how much to say about David's connection to Clay – though Rita certainly knew about their relationship, she might not enjoy discussing it. But she saved me the trouble. "I'm glad Clay has teamed up with David," she said, no uneasiness in her voice. "It's made a big difference. I doubt he would have risked this new video line unless things were ... well, stable at home."

I pretended to a knowledge I didn't have. "Yes, I think they're getting along really well."

"It was that trip to St. Louis, don't you think? It cemented things."

I put down my knife and fork. "What trip to St. Louis?"

"Oh dear." She put her hand to her cheek. "I assumed you knew."

"I had no idea."

A pause inserted itself. "I can ask David about it," I said, to get her off the hook. "Generally, we don't have any secrets."

"He thinks the world of you."

I held my tongue for a few moments, then it got away from me. "What happened in St. Louis, Rita?"

"Oh, Bruce." I could see her tact struggling with her loyalty. "I'm amazed David didn't tell you." More struggle and then, finally, "He got in some trouble and Clay went out to ... to help."

I could feel my heart thumping around. "Trouble with the police?"

She nodded. "I don't know the details. I think he had been indiscreet in some way. I'm sure it was due to stress, being away from home, playing in public ..."

"And Clay fixed it?"

"I'm not sure what he did. Found a lawyer or paid someone off. Anyway, they've been much closer since then."

I started to eat again. So that was it. David had gotten himself into a jam and Clay had gotten him out.

Rita relieved herself by changing the subject. She got onto the American novel. Apparently it had reached a peak of influence in 1926 and gone downhill ever since. But I hardly listened. Something else was stirring around in my gut.

Had David refused to tell the New York cops about Clay's presence in Miles's apartment *because he owed him one*? Because it was his way of paying Clay back for the rescue in St. Louis?

A sudden despair swept through me. I had been David Donnenfeld's confidant for almost ten years. I had heard all his griefs, his insecurities, his hopes and fantasies. It had been a form of love. And now I was on the outside looking in.

I felt Rita's dark eyes on me. She had stopped talking and was waiting for me to come around. At last she said, "There's a favor I want to ask you, Bruce. This lunch wasn't entirely social and altruistic." She gave her nervous laugh.

I was still put off, struggling with my hurt, but I managed to say something.

"My daughter would like to take music lessons. She's rather a special child."

The story came out slowly. I was able to focus in bits and pieces, and then wholly. Leslie Osterkamp was eighteen with a difficult childhood behind her. Joe Osterkamp had left them when Leslie was eleven, a particularly difficult age. "I never really understood why he left us," Rita said with a wan smile, "but my parents weren't surprised. I'd taken him down to Miami to meet them and they didn't like him at all. I thought it was the cultural difference, of course – I told my *papi* that if Joe loved me one-tenth as much as he did, I'd be fine – but they were right. Cubans have an instinct about these things. Later, my mother said she knew he was a *cabrón* from the very beginning."

"*A cabrón?*"

"A man who never stops ... playing around." She paused, collecting herself. "Anyway, I raised Leslie by myself. Whatever I did was wrong, of course. Too permissive or too restrictive. Too much love or not enough. Never the right amount at the right time."

She gave a deep sigh. "She changed schools a great many times. But last fall, after a lot of trouble, we got her into Bennington."

But it hadn't worked. Leslie had suffered a kind of collapse in the spring. Now she was home again, refusing to go back to college, sitting around the house.

"However," Rita went on, "there's a silver lining to all this. She's always written poetry and now she's started writing songs. Settings for her poems. She plays the guitar. She says this is her real career. I thought, well, it might be a way to get her moving again."

Years of experience came to my aid. "I've got just the teacher for her. Luddie Chametsky, my partner. He's wonderful with talented, disturbed kids. Half our students are slightly batty anyway. I'll talk to him. He can go over her stuff, then lead her into theory, ear training, arranging, whatever interests her."

Rita's face lit up. "That would be wonderful. I just know it's the right thing for her."

"Have her call me. I'll set it up with Luddie."

She shook her head. "I can't thank you enough."

I reached over and put my hand on hers. "We're always looking for new students. How do you think we pay our bills?"

But after putting her in a taxi on Spring Street, my demons began to rage again. Trouble in St. Louis, a flying rescue, home again to a tighter relationship. And now that David was in real trouble – not for screwing around in public but involving a homicide – some kind of misplaced loyalty was at work. David wouldn't defend himself even though not doing so put his career at risk.

§ § §

I arrived at the 20th Precinct at four o'clock the same afternoon, which was stretching my day. They were uptown, on West 82nd Street, near the apartment where Miles had lived. I noticed a plaque in the vestibule commemorating a number of patrolmen killed in the line of duty.

A burly sergeant sat behind the raised bench to the left. In an alcove a clerk was scribbling; in another, a man sat with earphones. The sergeant, whose name on the plaque was, appropriately, Traficante, examined me. "What do you want?"

None of the niceties of sales clerks here. "I want to talk to Detective Kerrison."

"What about?"

I hesitated. I didn't want my private business aired. An elderly couple had just entered behind me. "About the Miles Halloran case. Detective Kerrison asked me to keep him posted on new developments."

Officer Traficante stared at my clothes, then into my eyes. Apparently I passed muster, because he motioned to a bench, first taking my name and address and phone. Then he stared at the elderly couple. They had just been mugged in Central Park, by the lake at 77th Street. They were still giving the details in outraged tones when I was called inside.

I stumbled a couple of times walking back, steadying myself against the tiled wall. Zinsser had warned me against stress. I couldn't imagine anything more stressful than this. I was about to betray a friend.

Kerrison was standing at the back of a windowless little office. On his desk was a Compaq Deskpro 386, the monitor blank. We shook hands and he motioned me to a chair. My eye strayed to the computer. Had it been employed in Miles's case? Patterns of violence? M.O.'s? Fingerprints? Somehow I doubted it.

"You told me to contact you if I had any new information."

He sat down. "Shoot."

Now that the moment was here I wasn't really ready. "Miles had an apartment in Puerto Rico. On the beach. Fairly expensive."

Kerrison shuttered down his eyes. "We know that."

"Before that he lived in a much less expensive place. Kind of ratty, in fact." I paused. "I got a call from one of his friends down there. Miles was mixed up with some shady characters. He thinks you should check it out."

A sigh, denoting weariness.

"I brought his name and phone for you." I pushed the slip of paper forward. It had Sonny Barowski's name and address. "He said he'd be glad to help in any way. I think he knows something ..." I trailed off.

"This crime took place in New York City."

"There are flights to Puerto Rico every few hours." I tried to keep the sarcasm out of my voice.

He didn't react. "We liaise with the police down there. I'll see if they want to follow up."

I recalled something Barowski had said just before ringing off. "He said not to talk to the local cops, they're hopelessly corrupt."

Kerrison didn't like that. He stared at me. "This type of murder is pretty common, Dr. Pittman."

"What type is that?"

"Well ... the lifestyle-type murder."

"You mean gay?"

"That's what I mean."

He didn't look at me, sparing me the embarrassment, no doubt. "We tend to enjoy the company of people who are like us," I said, "that doesn't mean Miles consorted with murderers."

"There were no signs of forced entry. He let the perpetrator in the house."

That was my cue. It was time to tell Kerrison that Clay Lemaitre was the third party they were seeking. But I still wasn't quite ready. "I think you should call Sonny Barowski. Or, if you trust them, fax the details of the case to the investigators down there."

He nodded. Again the words I had come to speak rose to my tongue. Kerrison was fidgeting, leaning forward. He was bored, disinterested. And then it hit me – he didn't care about Miles's death. It wasn't high on his list of priorities. Justice, like good medical care, went to those with clout or money. The Halloran case was the equivalent, in Kerrison's lexicon, of a drug dealer getting offed in a drive-by shooting. No big deal. Why should I give him a break? Why should I compromise Clay, and by extension, David?

"Anything else you care to pass on?"

I stood up. "No, nothing at all."

He walked me down the hall, almost to the front door. When I hit the street, I saw that my Puerto Rico tip would be filed and forgotten. Too far away, too inconvenient. My errand had been a total failure.

In the taxi going home I was chilled. All the windows were closed, but I still felt icy. I hobbled into my building. An early winter wind was whipping up from the river. As I put my key in the front lock, it occurred to me that the elderlies were blowing tonight – gusts bringing age and depletion.

Ten minutes after I got inside, the phone rang. It was David.

"What the hell happened to you? I haven't heard from you for a week."

"I'm sorry, Bruce. Some funny things have been going on."

I could feel a brief surge of energy. Or was it merely curiosity? "What kind of things?"

"Well ..." his voice became cautious. "Yesterday afternoon, late, I got a call from Kings' Hospital in Brooklyn. They said my sister Esther was going into emergency surgery. They said she'd been sideswiped by a car crossing Eastern Parkway, near the Brooklyn Museum."

He cleared his throat. "I dropped everything and hit the subway. I was due at the Philharmonic to hear Shirley, but I figured I had time. But when I got to the hospital, they had no record of Esther Bergmann – that's her married name – being admitted. I went racing around for hours. I looked in the emergencies and the ICUs and the wards and clinics till 8 o'clock. I figured they had checked her in, but there'd been a clerical slip-up. That hospital is the pits."

I knew that Kings' Hospital was often lethal.

"Finally, I didn't know what to do so I called Esther's house. I should have done it first thing. You won't believe this, Bruce, she answered the phone. The whole thing was a hoax."

I tensed, full of premonitions.

"By the time I got back to Manhattan it was ten o'clock, and I'd missed Shirley's performance. I really felt crummy. I saw the review this morning, but I haven't been able to reach her."

I exhaled in relief. Nothing disastrous.

"When I was going out of the house late this morning, the super told me there'd been a break-in on my floor. While I was at the hospital. I'm in 6-A. Somebody broke into 6-E. I don't know them, they moved in a few weeks ago." He sputtered nervously. "I don't know whether that was a coincidence or what."

"Of course it's a coincidence. Was anything taken?"

"Yeah, some electronic gear," he said.

"Then there's no connection between your trip to the hospital and the break-in. It was just a standard New York burglary." I paused. "You still didn't tell the police about Clay being on the premises." I tried not to sound accusatory.

"No. Not yet."

"You said you would."

"I know, Bruce ..." I could almost see his body twisting away from the phone. "I will, just give me a little time."

"Time." I echoed the word sarcastically. "I just hope

we have all of it we need."

Our goodbyes were a little cool. Somewhere, in the distance, I could hear the bonds of our contract, the one we had forged a decade ago, snapping. But we promised to keep in touch.

LESLIE OSTERKAMP WAS WAITING in my office the next day. She was tall like her mother, but fair-haired and without the olive tint to her skin. I thought I saw an expression of panic deep in her eyes.

"Mother says you have AIDS," was her opening remark.

I got up and closed the door. "Leslie, if you go around saying that, we're going to lose half the student body."

"I know." She didn't smile, just kept her terror-stricken eyes on me. "I just wanted to say it out loud." She tossed her head slightly. "Don't worry, I'm good at secrets."

She looked younger than eighteen, but she was probably older in unsuspected ways. "I feel good most days, I do my work, I try not to obsess."

She nodded. "My best friend at Euthanasia was gay."

"At where?"

"Youth in Hastings. It's a school for problem kids in Westchester. We always called it Euthanasia. I went there after they kicked me out of St. Timothy's." She paused. "His name was Jimmy Kanner, I hope he's okay."

Time to change the subject. "Your mother says you write beautiful songs."

"How does she know? I never play them when she's home."

"Maybe she guessed. I hope you're going to play them for us. We're going to skip the usual audition, on your mother's recommendation."

She winced slightly. She was watching for over-compensation, the bane of problem children. She really wanted to be treated exactly like everybody else. I backtracked. "Of course, you'll have to play something for your teacher here, Mr. Chametsky. He's very busy, he doesn't take just anybody."

She perked up right away. "I don't mind." She reached down and touched her case. "I brought my guitar."

I went to the door and across the hall. Luckily, Luddie was in his office. He was on the phone, trying to set up a master class in song accompaniment with Warren Valente. I heard them agree on a three-session series. A coup for us. He followed me back. He had been briefed about Leslie.

I noticed, not for the first time, that Luddie expanded in the presence of difficult girls, especially if they were attractive. Now, looking at Leslie Osterkamp through his eyes, I could see that she was quite beautiful. Delicate features, pale skin, a full, sensual figure. She might have been more alluring, I thought, if she hadn't been wearing unclean jeans and a black leather jacket, but the signals had come through to Luddie. His eyes had gone a little smoky.

"Where did you learn to write songs, Leslie?"

Leslie wriggled with pleasure. "I taught myself."

"Some of the best do that," Luddie went on, "but that doesn't mean they can't pick up some new ideas. Can I hear what you've done?"

I saw the panic again, briefly, then it was quelled and she stood up. I thought I heard a harp-like sound coming from Luddie's solar plexus as they left.

Ten minutes later he returned. "She can't read music, Bruce."

I let out a low whistle.

"Do we really want to take on a composition student who doesn't know bass from treble?"

"We've had beginners before."

"This girl has all kinds of learning disabilities, I can tell."

I thought about my promise to Rita. "Can't you work with her?"

He didn't answer.

"Does she have any talent?"

"Tons, like everybody else around here."

It was true, the school was lumpy with talent. "I suggest a compromise then. You take her for comp. I'll get Hank Lilienthal to take her for an intensive in notation. We'll put her in the History of Music course, too."

Luddie studied the top of my head for a while. "I have a feeling she won't last but ... what the hell." His disinterest sounded a trifle forced. I'd never known him to take on a student he didn't believe in. But I let it pass. "I'll tell her," he said, heading out.

I ran into Leslie an hour later in the snack-machine area that passed for a student lounge. She was talking with some kids her own age. While I waited for the robot inside the coffee machine to serve me, she came over. "He's cute," she said.

"Who?"

"Luddie. That's what he told me to call him."

It was a perfect opening for a little lecture on the

virtues of perseverance and self-discipline, but in a moment of inspiration I held my tongue. Soon enough she'd find out how Luddie worked – his professionalism, his refusal to tolerate laziness, his tenacity.

I simply said we were glad to have her in the school.

§ § §

Roosevelt Hospital, at 58th Street, is a set of ancient red brick buildings encrusted with time and pain. I'd gotten the call about Tim Currier a couple of days ago, but hadn't found the energy, or courage, to visit until now. I had known he was infected – we kept in touch – but was informed of his sudden deterioration by his current lover, Simon Moran. They had hooked up after Tim moved out of my old loft on 18th Street.

When we met, Timothy Currier was a teacher in the New York public school system – a strange choice for a young man from Skowhegan, Maine. Or maybe not so strange; he always claimed teaching was a lower-middle-class profession. His parents were millworkers, but he had gotten scholarships to Exeter and Yale, then began his lifelong collection of useless facts. "You want to be loved for knowing things," I used to say, after he had filled me in on botany, political economy, the history of the Inquisition, the chemistry of baking. He would deny it, saying he was merely curious, and that if I had a more broad ranging intellect my life wouldn't be spent at the bottom of a well.

"There's music down that well," I would reply, which would send him into a diatribe on the flaws of over-specialization. I suppose we were basically incompatible – me with my inward focus, Tim with his ever-widening range, but we were in our thirties and a steady partner was essential. We lasted five years. He went on to Simon Moran and I went on to marry the Longacre Music School.

He was in a room by himself with a fine view of an airshaft. He lay on his back, staring at the ceiling, an oxygen mask on his face. His robe was disheveled. I could see that his skin was translucent and his bones were glowing.

"How you doin', Tim?" I bent over the bed.

He smiled and made a winding motion. I raised the bed. Then I helped adjust the oxygen mask. The vapor hissed as it entered the mask. He had to lift it each time he spoke. A tray sat on the table alongside, the food untouched.

"You're not eating?"

"Can't. They asked me if I wanted anything ..." He lowered the mask to inhale some air, "... and I said chocolate pudding." A square of pudding, uneaten, gleamed darkly on the tray.

"Do you want to try it now?"

He shook his head. "I could eat some pizza but they don't have it."

"I can get you some."

"In a minute." I waited. "I want you to call the Met."

"Who?"

"The opera. Look up the number. Ask for Phoebe Adams. Tell her I can't ..." he flipped down the mask again and breathed, "...can't be in *Don Carlos* next week, I'm sick."

I remembered – he had subbed as a spear-carrier in a couple of productions recently. He said he wanted to understand the tech side of a great opera house, even though he hated opera.

"Surely if you don't show up ..."

He shook his head angrily, then lifted the mask. "I don't want her to think I copped out."

"Okay, I'll call her as soon as I get home."

But he shook his head again. "Now." He pointed to his phone. He held up three fingers. "I do three scenes in *Don Carlos*, two costumes."

I lifted the phone. It took a while, the hospital switchboard reluctant to connect me to Information, but at last it was done. I watched Tim as I talked to the Met. After I hung up, I said, "The Met sends love and hopes you get well soon."

That seemed to please him. "The Met sends love," he whispered behind the mask.

"I can get that pizza now, you want anything on it?"

He didn't reply. His eyes were closed. I sat for a while watching him. I imagined the virus working its way down his spine. No one could predict which bodily system it would destroy first.

I stood up. "I'll get it plain," I said, too loudly. He opened his eyes briefly.

When I returned with the pizza, he was sound asleep. The paramedic, a heavy woman in a pink outfit, told me she'd hold the food and reheat it later. I never found out if he asked for it. When I called the next day he was on a respirator and three days later he died. He was 43. There were hundreds, maybe thousands, of things he still wanted to learn, although by now he probably had the answer to the biggest question of all.

§ § §

I had never been inside the Harvard Club, though I had passed it, on 44th Street just off Fifth, many times. Clay, I recalled, had gone to the B-school.

The elderly attendant at the door, perhaps spotting me as an interloper, pointed to the coat check and to a bulletin board. It was made out of those white plastic letters they use in crummy restaurants for the day's specials. One of them said LIGHTNING BOOKS – Lowell Room. The old man pointed up the stairs.

I trudged up slowly, holding onto the banisters. Stairs were hard for me these days. On the way up I caught a fleeting glimpse of the bar area downstairs and, beyond, a vast hall decked with flags and animal heads. A little corner of Teddy Roosevelt's America congealed by time and money.

I saw Rita first. She came over and gave me a hug. She was wearing a black cocktail dress with tiny bows here and there. "I'm so glad you came, Bruce," she squeezed her eyes with pleasure. "Leslie talks about her school all the time."

I nodded, trying not to look pleased.

After two weeks, Leslie still had a long way to go.

"Where's Clay?" I asked.

"He's over there talking to someone from PW." I saw him, wearing a brown tweed suit and a velvet vest of forest green. Suitably literary for the occasion.

As if reading my mind, Rita said, "We don't know if we need help from the book people or the TV people or the movie people. Maybe all three."

"Well, from what I hear, you ought to be grateful for anything. Romances aren't exactly news these days."

An ungracious remark. She looked at me reprovingly. "Romances on videos are almost new, Bruce. Come on."

She took me to a table in the center of the room, where three cassettes were displayed. *The Pirate's Return* showed a young man with piercing green eyes and a gold hoop in one ear, menacing a full-breasted young lady in a hoopskirt. I turned to Rita. "What's this for, the S&M market?"

But she excused herself – more new arrivals. I continued my examination of the titles.

A Savage at Sunset depicted an English manor. In the foreground a young man in riding boots was brandishing a wicked-looking crop at a young woman on a bench. More sadism, I thought.

The Ghost Dancers of Rue was even sillier. A woman on a distant stage was striking poses, while in the foreground a handsome young man in black tights and a cutaway white shirt was observing her. There were cobwebs everywhere.

"Bruce." Clay extended his hand. "Rita said you might come. It's good to see you."

"Well, I appreciate the invitation. I don't get to the Harvard Club every day."

"Well, these book parties are mostly a ritual. But we like to fill them up with interesting people." He looked around. "Some of our authors are here, would you like to meet any of them?"

My eye went back to *The Ghost Dancers of Rue*. I could see now that the woman on-stage was actually dancing. "That one's kind of intriguing."

"It's by Glinda Collins, one of our best. Come on."

He led me across the room to a woman in her fifties, wearing harlequin glasses. Her hair was grey and severely cut. She obviously had the same hairdresser as Prince Valiant. After introducing me, Clay wandered off.

"Are you a writer?" inquired Miss Collins.

"No. A musician."

"That's good. Writing is a terrible business. If you ever decide to take it up, I'd advise you to buy one of those novel-writing programs. It will save you a world of trouble."

She laughed and tossed down her drink. She seemed to have a good outlook on life. "Is Glinda a *nom de plume*?" I asked.

"Of course it is. You don't think my parents gave me a monicker like that?"

"Isn't she a character in the Oz books?"

"Glinda the Good saved Dorothy from no end of trouble. I never came across a writer named Glinda so I decided that's for me. In this business you have to stand out."

"And you wrote the video about the ballet dancers."

"I wrote it first as a novel. It sold so well Clay decided to convert it to video. I had my doubts right along but he has enough faith for multitudes." She snagged another drink from a passing tray.

"*The Ghost Dancers of Rue*, that's a nice title." I was running out of small talk. "What's Rue?"

"Rue is the name of a mysterious chateau in the south of France. You may think the word is French for street, but actually it refers to a plant. Rue-de-chèvre, goat's rue, which grows wild on the chateau grounds."

She must have noticed my discomfort because she said, "If you want to take a cassette, I'll autograph it for you."

No sooner said than done. I took a cassette from the pile. She wrote on the cover, obscuring the young man's chest. I put it under my arm and headed for the buffet, wondering what delicacies my stomach could tolerate this afternoon. Rita caught up with me there.

"I saw you talking to one of our authors."

"Glinda the Good. We both loved the Oz books, apparently. Did you know that Glinda had a mirror she could look into and see anything happening in her kingdom just as it happened?"

"My God, it sounds like CNN."

"Also a book that wrote out things at the exact moment they occurred?"

Rita smiled. "Now there's a publishing idea I like."

I laughed. "Are all your authors like Glinda?"

"She's one of the jollier ones. She doesn't take herself too seriously. Some of them, especially the men who write in twos, are impossible."

I motioned to the cassette table. "You mean some of those are written by men?"

"Of course. That's Rosemary Renfrew right over there. *The Pirate's Return*."

I saw a middle-aged male pair deep in conversation with a member of the fourth estate – at least I judged that from the notebook she was writing in. I couldn't resist. "Which one is Rosemary and which one is Renfrew?"

"Now Bruce." She tapped me on the arm. "Do you want to meet them?"

I took a step backward. "I'll introduce myself later."

As Rita moved off, I wondered if I might indulge in a drink. I was just about to signal a waiter when an elderly lady, smiling softly, came into my line of vision. She was wearing a beige outfit, topped by a pork-pie hat with a curling red feather. The general impression was of Robin Hood.

"My name is Polly Alvarado," she said, in a surprisingly strong voice. "Rita tells me you're a friend of Miles Halloran."

I introduced myself, though she seemed to know my name.

"Are you ill?" she peered at me.

The usual dilemma. "I'm not in the best of health."

"My husband was a physician. He said to look at the

eyes. Eyes first."

I blinked. That was a new one.

"I don't wish to pry. I simply wish you a speedy recovery."

I thanked her, wondering who had told her.

"I was quite upset by the news of Miles," she went on. "I didn't hear it until a few days ago. We're sheltered from that sort of thing in Old Saybrook."

"I guess the tabloids don't get that far."

"They do, I just don't read them."

"How did you find out, if I may ask?"

"Betty Jean Collins told me. She keeps up on all the violent crimes."

When I didn't react, she said, "Glinda. She's an old friend and neighbor. I knew her before she became a character in an Oz book."

"Do you read her stories, Mrs. Alvarado?"

"Heavens no. They're for shopgirls."

The Victorian phrase made me smile. "They're also for lawyers, accountants, computer programmers and members of Congress, if you believe the publishers."

"What nonsense."

I had the impression of a lifetime spent speaking her mind. "May I ask if you knew Miles for a long time?"

"I met him a month ago, actually. In Greece. I had a fall on the Acropolis – there are an amazing number of stones lying about – and he rescued me. We went through both museums together and then he put me in a taxi. I invited him to come for tea at the Grande Bretagne. We got together several times and had a wonderful outing to Aegina one day. I thought he had great character. He was always himself."

"He was that."

"You appreciate it as this country becomes more

homogenized." She looked around the room. "Everyone is always trying to sell you something. Themselves, if they don't have anything more useful."

I could see why she and Miles had hit it off.

"Have the police found anything?" she asked.

"I don't think they've been looking very hard."

"It's odd," she went on, "I had the impression he was expecting trouble of some sort."

I looked around. The party had thinned out a bit.

"Of course, his tastes were rather special," she added. "I assumed his worries were related to that. But he seemed preoccupied, even in Greece, where I think he was perfectly safe."

"When was the last time you saw him, Mrs. Alvarado?"

"He went off to Hydra for a few days and I left for Rome. We promised to get together back in the States." She drew her breath in sharply. "One more gone." The darkness became visible to her for a moment, then she collected herself. "I have to rescue Betty Jean before she makes more of a fool of herself. That's why I'm here." She put out her hand. "Come and see me in Old Saybrook."

I watched her move toward Glinda. By some alchemy of lighting, Glinda's hair had turned from grey to mauve and her harlequin glasses were gleaming like windows at sunset. Her novel/video was heavy under my arm and my tolerance for this party had just about evaporated. I recalled Milton's remark about books, a legend inscribed over the door to the reading room at 42nd Street: "A good book is the precious life-blood of a master spirit." I doubted that the romance under my arm was anybody's precious life-blood.

I found Clay and Rita and made my goodbyes. On my way out I passed Rosemary and Renfrew talking *sotto voce* to an older man in a blue pinstripe. "I love to suck," the man in the pinstripe was saying, "but it gives me gas."

One of the romance writers gave a porcelain leer. "Why don't you take out your teeth like I do?" he asked.

I fled down the stairs.

On the way downtown in a taxi one of Polly Alvarado's remarks echoed in my ears: *He was always himself.* She had said it about Miles and now it struck me as a tremendous compliment. It was, I realized, one reason I had always been drawn to him – Miles made no concessions to expectation, popular taste, prejudice. He was always himself.

I couldn't help comparing that judgment to my perception of Clay Lemaitre at the party. He had been all smoothness, suavity, courtesy. That was his job, of course, and the reason for his success. Yet his manner, his practiced duplicity, enabled him to deny his behavior with David to the police. You'd never know he was withholding evidence – that, in fact, he was an accessory, or at least a material witness, to Miles's murder. It might never have happened. Clay, I thought, was never himself.

I still hadn't decided on the next step. Whether to bring more pressure to bear on David, to pay another call on Kerrison, or forget the whole thing.

It was a well-worn circle, and by the time I got home I was sick of it all over again. Inside the house, I put Glinda Collins's video/novel on the TV and started fixing dinner. No El Paso chili tonight – I was going to have some of Angela's health food. Tofu, sunflower seeds and pasta – a combination that would have made me throw up a few months earlier.

After dinner I remembered the cassette. I picked it up and looked at the cover art again. It was really quite sexy. I turned it over and began to read the back copy.

What is the secret of the Chateau de Rue, where the reclusive Marquise de Norpois lives with a fiery young man whom she has trained to be her partner in the great classical ballets? What happens when a young American woman enters this eerie world and comes between the French noblewoman and her handsome protegé? In a vivid drama of intrigue and rivalry, we watch passions blaze into a conflagration that destroys some and heals others. Starring Sterling Roberts as Pierre, Ana de Meilhac as the Marquise, Marian Minton as Carolyn ...

I felt the brush of something familiar as I read, then dismissed it. It was like a phrase of music you couldn't quite place – useless to chase after it. I put the cassette down and flicked on the evening news. I wouldn't screen that junk tonight. I was in no mood for blazing passions or vivid intrigues.

The phone rang about an hour later. It was Sonny Barowski in Puerto Rico again. It had been several weeks since we spoke, he pointed out, and he'd heard nothing more. What was happening?

I explained about passing on his information to the people in charge of the Halloran case, and their lack of interest. "All those cops are alike," he snarled, "they won't follow up until an informant pops out of a file cabinet."

"They've probably closed the case by now," I replied. "Nothing new coming in, no pressure from the media." I didn't mention their hounding of David.

"Well, there's something new down here. My friend Ocasio Flores, who works with me on *The Star*, told me Miles was making regular trips to Grand Cayman."

"What for?"

"Well, that's the question. It certainly wasn't for him-self. Grand Cayman means numbered accounts, banking privacy, no IRS, the whole bit. It's a regular little Switzerland."

I couldn't help chuckling. "Who would ask Miles to do that? He was terribly conspicuous."

Barowski snorted. "They couldn't ask for a better courier. Nobody would suspect him. He was a joke wherever he went. Dyed hair, eye shadow, outrageous clothes, everything. They probably peeled off a grand for him after each trip." He paused. "I'm telling you, Bruce, the solution is down here."

A feeling of helplessness went through me. "I don't know what I can do about all this, Sonny."

"Maybe the two of us could take on these bastards."

"That's out of the question right now."

"That's what they're counting on. Nobody gives a damn."

"Sonny, we wouldn't even know where to begin."

"Ocasio has some good connections. I've got some friends. We can start there."

I began to say I was too sick but checked myself. I hated hearing the change in people's voices. At last I said I'd have to get back to him. The conversation ended on a sour note.

Sleep came quickly, as it always did these days, in spite of all the complications pressing on me. In fact, maybe because of them. Sleep, oblivion, was really the only solution, the only way to keep all the nightmares at bay.

G USTAVE KATZ HAD A SET OF golden ears, which he kept plugged with cotton. I had seen him weep when a fire engine went by. Today, Gustave, who liked pastry as well as music, loomed over my desk.

"Bruce, it is perhaps too much to ask that we give grades that mean something? Can we give once in a while an F?"

Gustave's mastery of tones did not extend to English word order. "If you want to fail them, Gustave, you need a reason, that's all."

It was an old faculty complaint. We had an arrangement with Pace College. Students in our degree program could take academic courses there, music courses with us. Pace would award the degree, after grading them strictly. But our teachers were softies, all except Katz. Bad grades at Longacre meant, maybe, no degree from Pace.

"I have two," he wiggled his fingers, "who do not know sonata form from *wiener schnitzel*."

"Did you give a final exam?"

"In Advanced Composition you write an advanced

composition. This is the exam."

"And?"

"These two, my eight-year-old granddaughter could do better."

"We don't expect our kids to be Mozart, Gustave."

"Mozart could do better while he was still inside his mother."

"Well..." If Gustave flunked them there would be outcries. "If you're sure ..."

"Bruce, would I give you a bum steering?"

I watched him lumber off, moaning gently and pressing the cotton in his ears. But school affairs seemed remote this morning. Whether Gustave flunked two students was far down my list of priorities. Before he turned up, I'd been wondering if I should notify Detective Kerrison about Barowski's call last night. Tell him Miles had been carrying cash to Grand Cayman. Now, after mulling it over, I decided against it. His reaction would surely be as before – major disinterest. If Miles had been running drug money it was a matter for the DEA or the Treasury, not the NYPD.

I was interrupted by a light tap on the door, though it was ajar as usual. It was Leslie Osterkamp, but with a difference. The punk clothes, tangled hair and colorful makeup were gone. She was wearing a soft chamois jacket over a pink tank-top and good jeans. "You look nice," I mumbled, waving her to a chair.

"How are you, Dr. Pittman?" She peered at me.

"To tell you the truth, I'm having a poor morning."

"I was reading about macrobiotic diets." She proceeded with the usual details. I interrupted her to say that most of the people on macrobiotics were dead.

"What do you have to lose?"

I was tired of that challenge too and showed it. She

changed the subject. "I want to sign up for the Pace program," she said.

"You mean you want to go for a degree?" When she nodded, I mentioned SAT scores, grade transcripts, recommendations, a few other things. Also an auto-biographical essay.

She knew all that. "I took the SAT a year ago when I applied to Bennington. I did okay. And I already started the essay." She looked down. "I'm not sure they're going to be real pleased with my recent activities."

"Well, Pace isn't Bennington, they probably expect a certain amount of ... urban upheaval."

"I'm being really honest," she went on. "I've already written about 75 pages, half a floppy disk. It just started pouring out." She paused. "I got so carried away last weekend I grabbed one of my mother's office files and wrote over it. She was furious."

I thought of Rita, probably the meticulous type when it came to her computer records. "I hope it wasn't their bookstore billing."

"Oh no." Leslie sighed. "It was one of those awful romances. An outline or a plot or something. She said I had lost a masterpiece, can you believe it? I did every-thing I could to retrieve it, but it was gone." She sighed again, then giggled. "Nobody will know what happened to Prince Alexey and the beautiful Berenice."

She glanced at her watch. "I have solfège class in a minute. I just wanted to ask ... is it okay about Pace? Would you write the letter of recommendation?"

"Of course."

She got up, slinging her leather bag over her shoul-der. "You're really cool, Bruce."

I watched her bounce out. I had been manipulated of course. I shouldn't be writing letters for a student of a few weeks. But what could I say? Besides, we were here to take chances on the young.

As soon as I was alone, my thoughts reverted to a familiar groove. What had Barowski said? *Maybe the two of us could take on these bastards.* Was he drunk when he said it? Boasting? He was the reckless type, Miles had said. He had a bullet scar in his leg. He'd found a local kid crawling up his *reja* and shot him. There had been retaliation, leading to an ambush in his driveway. Sonny and his wife had to leave the neighborhood, Trujillo Alto. Nobody had been killed, but almost. Was he a suitable partner in a crime investigation? Was *anyone* a suitable partner for an ailing music administrator with one lung on hold and the other heading for permanent vacation? I shook my head slowly. I'd been watching so many crime shows I couldn't distinguish art from reality.

By mid-afternoon all that was irrelevant. David Donnenfeld had been arrested and charged with the murder of Miles Halloran.

I heard the news when Erica came into Room 309 at 2:45, where my lesson with Emily Warshow was in progress. Behind Erica, I saw Shirley Scott and several others. David's attorney, Jim Slade, had called. David was in the Tombs. The D.A.'s office had told the press that new facts in the ongoing investigation had led to the charge.

I sat for a long moment, stunned, thinking about David, his family's reactions, and the odds of his being displayed, in handcuffs, on the Six O'Clock News.

I called Slade as soon as I got downstairs, clipping the rest of Emily's lesson. He said the police, armed with a search warrant, had entered David's apartment early this morning, without advance warning and before he was out of bed. "It's one of their tricks," Slade advised, "like the Gestapo or the KGB. Surprise helps." He paused.

"I don't know how they persuaded the judge they had probable cause. I haven't seen the warrant and I don't know which judge signed it. But they claim to have found some incriminating material."

My palms were wet against the receiver. "What kind of material?"

"As far as I can tell, and this is unverified, they found some written death threats."

"Are you kidding? David would never threaten Miles Halloran."

"I'm telling you what they claim they found, Bruce. It's flimsy and circumstantial. Whether it's a device to scare him, or smoke out another culprit, I don't know. We'll have to wait. I only found out this from a reporter I happen to know. The D.A.'s office never publicizes details before an arraignment."

"I can't believe I'm hearing this."

Slade's voice got cooler as mine rose. "Our first job is to get him out on bail. In maybe a couple of days. They tend to throw up roadblocks when there's a capital crime involved. But there should be no problem. Clay has agreed to put up whatever they require and we'll find a bondsman for the rest."

I was getting confused. "Can I see him?"

"He's in the holding area. No visitors."

"What about phoning?"

"He can only make a couple of calls a day, if he's lucky and if the phone is free. If he calls you, fine. If not, you'll have to check with me. He's permitted to keep in touch with me – they have to provide him with access."

I started in on the written death threats again but Slade interrupted. He'd told me all he knew. Finally he cut me off in mid-sentence, telling me he'd keep in touch.

I sat in a fog trying to find a way through this maze.

Death threats from David to Miles? Impossible. I let my imagination skip through the labyrinth. I recalled something Polly Alvarado had said at the video party. *I had the impression he was expecting trouble of some sort.* What was Miles involved in? Some kind of half-assed operation, the product of his bizarre imagination? The trips to Grand Cayman, the rough crowd he knew, the purchase of an expensive apartment on the beach – was any of that relevant? The fact that they had found some written death threats in David's possession meant nothing. They might have gotten there in a half- dozen ways, including a police plant. It wouldn't be the first time.

I wasn't getting anywhere. Erica and Shirley and Luddie had to be told of these new developments. I would have to reassure David's mother and sister too. I didn't want them hearing about it through the media.

And there was one more call to be made – one more revelation. I should have done it weeks ago, of course.

§ § §

I had trouble getting through to Kerrison at the 20th. Even though I left messages three times, he didn't return the calls. I was no longer useful to him. It wasn't amateur time any more.

Finally, on the fifth attempt, I got through. I spoke my piece quickly, efficiently. I'd had plenty of time to rehearse. I told the facts as I knew them. Clay Lemaitre had arrived at the Halloran apartment about ten p.m. on Monday, September 15. David and Miles were finishing dinner. Clay smoked a Schimmelpenninck cigar and had a nightcap. He and David left together about eleven p.m. Why they had kept this information from the authorities I didn't know, but it proved one thing: Miles had been alive when David left the apartment. There was now a witness.

Kerrison let me finish. I could picture his satisfaction at my little recital. Finally he spoke.

"We've known that for a while, Dr. Pittman."

"You have? How?"

"Some evidence on the premises. Also we have a witness who saw them leaving together. The superintendent was bagging garbage on the sidewalk about eleven p.m. and made a positive ID."

"Well, doesn't that prove what I'm saying?"

"We believe David Donnenfeld returned to the apartment later. Alone. To perpetrate the crime."

"What would his motive be?"

"Financial. He owed Halloran a large sum of money. Halloran was demanding repayment."

"That makes no sense at all."

"We have documents to back this up."

"What documents?"

"I can't say."

"You're probably wrong in this, detective. You're making a serious mistake."

"We'll stick with our evidence, Dr. Pittman. Thanks for calling."

A click. The phone was dead. And I had been the one who told them Miles had financed David's education.

§ § §

"Pancakes or scrambled eggs, sir?"

The flight attendant was Puerto Rican. We smiled at each other. His teeth gleamed, as did the whites of his eyes. "The New Tahitians," Miles used to call them. "On their island their skin color is lambent and glowing, a sign of sexual vitality. It sings against the harshness of the sun. Take them away, put them in New York or Chicago and the glow fades. It's like removing Gauguin's women from those reds and yellows and blues."

We had been lying on the beach at the time, sipping rum from disemboweled coconuts. "I can't imagine why they ever leave this paradise," he went on.

"Jobs," I said.

"Oh, jobs," he waved his hand disdainfully. "Down here they can live on mangos and plantains and those wretched tubers of theirs."

"You mean they can live in picturesque malnutrition just for you?"

And so we had argued, lazily, selfishly, as we lolled on the beach lapping up rum. My hypocrisy had been greater than Miles's. At least he approved of colonial exploitation; I was profiting from it while being morally superior.

"Here you go, sir." The pancakes were slid in front of me, a rubbery mound. I looked up. The handsome flight attendant oozed understanding. We smiled again. In another lifetime I would have made a beach date. Not now.

I tried to dismember the top pancake with a small plastic fork, obviously designed for cutting air. It broke. I wasn't hungry anyway.

Dr. Zinsser, whom I had called two days ago, not long after hearing the news of David's arrest and making the airline reservation, had not been pleased. "What kind of wild goose chase is this?" he'd asked.

"It's not a goose chase, it's something I have to do for a student. An ex-student."

"Can't you send someone else? Your immune system is compromised. You can't go running around the world."

"I'll be careful. I wonder if you'd call my druggist. I'm out of pills." I named several.

He grunted, told me to stay out of the sun, and hung up. But the medication was waiting at the apothecary's.

I glanced at my seat mate, an elderly woman who had crossed herself three times as we lifted off. Later she told me she had worked as a machine operator for 35 years, stitching luggage linings. Now she was going home to Cupey. She showed me pictures. They all lived in a small concrete box. I had a strong sense of the chasm that separated us, that separated me from all the passengers – PRs and continentals – heading for the island in holiday spirits.

A moment of fear swept over me. I hadn't slept much last night, and predictable symptoms were the result – a slight sore throat, shortness of breath, a hint of fever. My old friends, waiting to pounce. I closed my eyes. I'd try to sleep now.

But sleep wouldn't come. My mind replayed an article in *The Star* which I had picked up at the airport. There had been an attack on a police precinct in Tierra del Puerto. A couple of grenades had been lobbed through the front door, some snipers in the housing project across the way had fired a few rounds through the precinct windows and a speeding car had sprayed the place with automatic fire. All carefully coordinated at three a.m. No arrests had been made. It was the Caribbean Wild West. *What was I doing here?*

And then, as it always did, sleep arrived unexpectedly. When I woke up we were circling over El Morro, the sea was bordered with coco palms and the white cubes of the condos stood up in the distance. For a brief moment I felt strong, and then I remembered.

§ § §

Sonny Barowski was smaller, whiter, drier. His limp was more pronounced too. The tropics hadn't rained their sweet juices on him. But of course he had to earn a living here, had to cope with the traffic jams, power failures, strikes, hurricanes, bugs, heat.

As we headed for the luggage area, I recalled one of Miles's theories about expatriates. He claimed they we were the same all over the world – and he'd tried Dubai, Tangier, Hong Kong, Rhodes and Tenerife. Living abroad, he claimed, camouflaged your deeper estrangements. Abroad you were an official foreigner, professionally alienated, but it was no longer your fault. It was part of your accepted status. Therefore you were off the hook. "Rather a neat solution," he had concluded, "go abroad and leave your unsuccess at home, along with the scars of your childhood, the terrors of your adolescence, the failure of your adult life. That's why you find English and Americans all over Europe and Africa, a permanent colony of drinkers and pederasts and failed artists and ne'er-do-wells. But of course they can blame it on the colony, the island, on being away from that wonderful place called home. Never on themselves."

I knew what had brought Miles to Puerto Rico – the sun and the boys and his general flamboyance. But I wasn't sure about Barowski. Maybe I'd find out before I left.

"Marie and I are going to rent a place in New Hampshire next summer," he said as we waited by the luggage belt. "We can't stand the humidity here in July and August. Makes my leg worse."

"How's Marie?" She was his second – or was it his third? – wife, a quiet woman and a good amateur pianist. We had played Mozart four hands.

"She's fine." He looked grim. "She wants to get out of

here too."

That was another feature of expatriates, Miles had pointed out – they were always eager to leave, but the next place was exactly the same.

Sonny's ancient Volvo was in the airport lot. As we walked there, under a blue-and-gold November sky, the tradewinds softening the heat, I had another rush of good health. But it didn't last. After we lurched off, entering the traffic jam, I began to cough. Barowski listened. "You bring a cold down with you?"

"Slight."

"The sun'll clear it up. Puerto Rico cures respiratory ailments in no time."

If only it would, I thought. I looked to the right. "My God, where's the ocean?"

"Behind those condos. They put up another dozen since you were here. They're even trying to move the Isla Verde cemetery so they can build some more."

I saw a Chinese wall of garish high rises, fast-food joints, surf shops, glitzy restaurants.

Sonny was a reckless driver, wheeling through tight scrapes, butting ahead when he could, hitting the marginal roads to gain an edge. I held on and listened. "I don't know what Miles was into exactly, but his situation here changed drastically in the last couple of years. Did you know that?"

"I knew he bought that apartment in the Condado. I stayed there last time I visited him."

"Before that he lived in a two-room hole on Calle Sánchez," he went on. I nodded. I remembered that one too. "A bad neighborhood. Paid forty dollars a month. If he wanted some daylight he had to open the front door. That's when we met him. Marie bought one of his paintings at the Casa Cristal."

"Well, he had a place in New York, so I guess he just needed a *pied-à-terre* here," I replied.

"Then why did he buy that expensive place on Ashford? He paid at least a hundred thousand for it."

I pictured that apartment, high-ceilinged and cool, with overhead fans and tiled floors. Miles had painted the four rooms in pastel shades – one lime, one rose, one lemon, one gray. "Just like the place I had in Madrid, across from El Buen Retiro," he had announced, giving me a tour. "Built in the reign of Isabela Segunda – the one in Madrid, I mean."

"He didn't get that kind of money from painting *flamboyán* trees or writing paperback novels," Sonny went on. "So where does that leave us? With another source of income and some shady friends."

"Who are these friends?"

"Cubans mostly. One of them owns a shop up here." He gestured ahead. "Casa Cristal. We'll go there later."

"And you think something illegal was involved?"

"I don't know, but there's an information gap I'd like to plug."

We were in the Old City now, threading our way through the narrow streets of blue cobblestones – stones brought over as ballast in the empty ships from Spain, ships that went home loaded with the wealth of the Indies. I was staying at El Convento and we were almost there.

"I should tell you, Sonny, the police have just made an arrest in the case."

He half-turned toward me. "Who?"

"A young man, someone Miles had known for years. One of my students too. David Donnenfeld."

"Never heard of him."

"There might be a message for me at the hotel. He

might be out on bail by now."

"Do you think they got the right guy?"

"I wouldn't be here if I did."

He looked satisfied. "Then we have our work cut out for us."

He pulled up in front of the handsome façade of El Convento. A few minutes later I was upstairs in a room filled with reproductions of heavy Spanish furniture. I had told Sonny I needed to rest. He and Marie would meet me here for a late lunch.

I was just reaching for the phone to call New York when it rang. It was David. I gave a yelp of recognition and relief. "Are you okay?"

"Oh, Bruce."

"You're out."

"This morning. Two and a half days to remember."

"No permanent damage. No broken fingers."

A sour laugh. "All the damage is in my head. I'll tell you about it when I see you."

I started to say something encouraging then stifled the urge. Maybe the damage *was* permanent – it was too soon to say. "I'm down here following some hot tips ... did Clay tell you?"

"He said you had a friend down there. A friend of Miles." David didn't sound enthused. "I hope you're not wasting your time."

He told me what had happened in New York. The police, on their raid of his apartment, had found a letter, in an envelope, addressed to Miles. It was on the night table next to David's bed.

Miles told David, on the evening they had dinner, that the letter had been slipped under his door during the afternoon, while he was visiting me at St. Vincent's. He found it on his return. It was the second threatening letter he had received. He passed it on to David. "It was a threat, in bad English," David said, "to kill him. It said, 'You know why.'"

"Why did Miles pass it on to you?"

"I don't know, really."

"Did he tell you what it was all about?"

"No. But you know Miles. He was perfectly capable of writing himself a letter like this, just to mystify his friends. So I didn't take it too seriously." He paused. "It was foolish of me to take it home with me. I should have left it on the coffee table at Miles's. The police matched the copy in my possession to the first death threat which they found in Miles's apartment when they searched it. They decided I had sent the first and was getting ready to send the second. Of course, my fingerprints were all over it at that point."

We both paused. At last David said, "What I don't understand, Bruce, is why Miles laid this on me. It's so thoughtless. He was always so considerate."

"I don't believe he did it on purpose. He must have believed they were empty threats."

"Maybe." A dim laugh. "I'll tell you about the Criminal Courts Building when you get back. You won't believe it."

I tried to sound cheerful. "When I get back with some proof."

"Yeah." His voice was fainter now. "I really appreciate what you're doing ... under the circumstances."

"I didn't really have a choice, David."

Another pause, and then his voice fainter than before. "I understand that, Bruce."

After hanging up I lay back and tried to clear my mind. Miles and David, an intergenerational duo, a model of its kind.

I recalled a chat with Miles, not many months

after David had first enrolled with us. "He has one or two things to overcome before he can come into his own," Miles had said. "His background in Brooklyn, of course. Luckily, Jews have great respect for the arts. It comes naturally. You might say the invention of monotheism was the greatest single artistic achievement in history."

"Did you tell David that?" I asked.

"Yes, we talk about these things. We have more in common than you realize. I was raised as a Catholic in England."

I hadn't known. Miles rarely talked of his early life, though I had gleaned certain impressions – upper-middle-class family, private tutors, tours of the Continent, a father who rarely worked, the loss of everything in the great Depression.

"I've always understood, if that's the right word, religious persecution. That's a bond between David and me. The English considered us Papists, capable of treason, gunpowder plots. We were still trying to assassinate Good Queen Bess and put Mary Stuart on the throne. I was constantly hounded in school. Every year when they burned Guy Fawkes I was sure they had me and my family in mind." He paused. "And my father sympathized with Home Rule for Ireland, and was called in for questioning at the magistrate's. Very humiliating, everybody heard about it, I was beaten again by the other boys. They were cheered on, of course, by the Anglican clergy."

I shook my head. I really had no idea that under Miles's debonair manner these things still rankled.

"That was before the present enlightened age, but I dare say the persecutions have just gone underground. They still distrust Catholics in England, no matter what you saw on *Brideshead Revisited*."

I recalled my own bullying at home and at school.

It seemed to be a universal need, and the reasons simply changed from culture to culture.

"I also wanted David to feel free about his sexual tastes," Miles said on another occasion. "He was saddled with guilt – one of Jehovah's gifts to His people, and quite unnecessary if you're a musician. Beethoven was fixated on his nephew. Schubert was a chicken hawk. Robert Schumann slept with his male roommates and, when he was hospitalized, wouldn't let Clara visit him. Tchaikovsky we all know about. Mussorgsky died in a homoerotic funk. To succeed in 19th-century Paris you had to let yourself be seduced by Saint-Saëns, if he wanted you. I haven't mentioned Ravel, Gershwin, Copeland and Virgil Thompson. So if you feel alone with your perversion, don't. Welcome to the Musikverein. And of course, I have not even *begun* on the performers."

I had to laugh. Miles had it down pat. It was probably a speech he had given many times. I had a feeling David had profited from it. How ironic now that David should be accused of Miles's murder – and that Miles had, unwittingly, set it up. Partners in persecution indeed.

§ § §

"I think I'll be naughty and have a frozen daiquiri." Marie Barowski looked at her husband.

"Go ahead. I'll stick with rum and tonic." He waved for the waiter. I was having a Perrier.

We were in the open-air patio of El Convento, converted to a restaurant, sitting next to a vivid wall foundation of Spanish tiles. Water poured musically from a lion's mouth, a high E-flat in the bassoons. This patio was where the original residents of El Convento – virgins of good family from Sevilla, Jaén, Salamanca, Badajoz –

had walked in the evening, calming their souls after the hazards of converting heathens. Right now, though, the area was filed with young couples in shorts, elderly pairs in cruisewear and a group of Japanese.

"It's good to see you, Bruce. I can't tell you how upset we were about Miles." Marie reached out and touched my hand. They were an odd match – Barowski so grim, his wife so warm. But under the glass jar which descends over all couples, I sensed a good fit. She calmed him down; he kept her from getting bored. She taught English part-time at a private academy, the Robertson School.

When the drinks came – Marie's daiquiri was a huge glass mounded with green ice – I mentioned that I had talked to David an hour earlier. "He's the prime suspect in the case," I explained to Marie. "They found, or planted, some incriminating evidence in his apartment. But there's no way he could have been involved."

Marie looked from me to her husband. "I don't know why either of you wants to do this. Miles was mixed up with some awful funny people."

Sonny eyed her. "You know why."

"That was a long time ago."

"I don't forget things." Sonny turned toward me. "I had an uncle, born in Poland around the turn of the century. He was a character. He'd shoot you if you did him wrong, and he never forgot a kindness. I take after him."

I waited, curiosity aroused. I recalled that Sonny had once referred to a favor Miles had done him. We all sipped our drinks.

"I might as well tell you," Sonny resumed. "About five years ago, not long after we'd met Miles, I was in a bar on Loiza Street. La Cuevita. The Little Cave. I shouldn't have been drinking there. Full of scum, addicts. Tattoos on every arm – the kind they give each other with blue pens in prison. Anyway, I made the mistake of flashing some money. Not much, about thirty dollars, but I was drunk and I'd forgotten they'd kill you for thirty cents, let alone thirty dollars in a place like that.

"Miles was still living in that hole on Sánchez, which wasn't far away, and he spotted me through the open doorway. He sized it up right away, walked in cool as you please, and eased me out before anybody knew what was happening. I wouldn't cooperate, too goddamn hard-headed – but he pushed me into a cab and got me home. Later I realized it was the kind of situation where you have to psych them out and do it fast. Miles was an expert at that."

I nodded. Marie continued to look distressed.

"When I woke up next morning, I realized what a favor he'd done me."

Marie interrupted. "A friend of ours, Harley McDivitt, was stabbed to death in a bar just a few doors down from La Cuevita."

"Yeah," Sonny went on, "the knife blade went in the side of his skull. He didn't even know he'd been hurt till he keeled over on the street." He paused. "So I owe Miles one. And goddam it, I'm gonna repay him."

A typical Miles maneuver, I thought – no physical strength, just quickwittedness and prompt action.

"I only told you this to explain things," Sonny said, "no need to spread it around."

I smiled quietly. "I won't tell a soul."

Over drinks we discussed some of Sonny's ideas, or intuitions, since none had any basis in fact. "Ocasio Flores told me that his contacts at the *cuartel general* – that's the police headquarters here – said Miles had been at El Barrilito when the Hacienda people raided it."

"What's El Barrilito?"

"A club run by Tupi Rivera, very handy to the docks. The passengers, the crews from the cruise ships, can stroll right over. Basically it's a house of prostitution. The scuttlebutt is that Tupi is connected to one of the crime families in New York."

I pointed out Miles's taste for low life, but Sonny cut me off. "El Barrilito isn't where you go for harmless sleaze."

"Why don't we order some lunch?" Marie offered. "I'm starving."

"There's also the question of Eduardo Conde," Sonny went on. "He handled Miles's paintings. It must have been Conde who made the contact with Tupi Rivera and sold him one of the canvases. What do you think of that?"

"Not much."

"He and Miles were good friends. I used to see them at the Tapia, at the Civic Theater or the film festivals." Sonny chewed his lower lip. I had the impression that Sonny was enjoying this. And why not? He was getting to play private eye.

"So we know that Miles was chummy with a Cuban named Conde," I said, "who served as his agent, and that a painting was sold to a questionable club, and that during a raid Miles Halloran was found on the premises. What does that add up to?"

"There's another item," Sonny went on. "Miles worked part-time in a souvenir shop at the Flamingo Hotel a couple of years ago. Before he came into his fortune. Worked for a Swiss woman, Heidi somebody. She accused him of not reporting all the sales he made. Threatened to bring charges."

"So?"

"Well, that testifies to his moral character. You've been sure Miles was some kind of saint. He wasn't."

"Even though he saved your life one night?"

"I don't think the two events are related."

I sighed, fighting the notion that I had made a terrible mistake in coming down here. "When am I going to meet your friend Ocasio Flores?" I asked.

"Tonight."

"I want the *ensalada de camarones*," Marie cut in. She laughed merrily. "Do you know, when I first came here, I thought that meant *salad of chambermaids*?"

§ § §

After lunch I decided to take a stroll. It was a part of town, the tip facing the harbor, that I knew well. To my left was the triple portal of the Cathedral, at the top of a hill that led down to the Main Gate. It was up to this hill that newly arrived voyagers climbed to give thanks for their safe arrival from Spain, to sing the Te Deum. I could picture them now, a half-starved procession of officers and priests, seamen and *cañoneros* and *arquebuceros*, their haggard faces reflecting the illusion that the New World would supply what the Old World had not. In the distance, above the gate, I could see La Fortaleza, the oldest fort in the city, now the governor's residence. It was there, I recalled, that the Spanish flag was lowered in 1898 and the U.S. flag went up. Now I could see the Puerto Rican flag flapping in the breeze. A pleasant sight.

I had first toured this quarter with Miles on my first visit, shortly after meeting him at the beach. He wasn't your typical guide. When I stopped to read the plaques and signs, he dragged me away. "Bruce, none of that is true. They're lies made up by the Turismo people and the Institute of Culture." Instead, he wanted me to observe the line of brown pelicans diving into the harbor, the mountains behind the town of Catano to the east, the little ferry boat crossing the bay.

He took me to one of his favorite spots – a little park at the foot of Calle San José overlooking La Princesa jail. The recreation yard for inmates, a small paved area, lay directly below us. The prisoners saw us right off. Maybe they knew Miles already, because some of them grabbed their crotches, whistled and cat-called. Miles, to my embarrassment, loved it. He fluttered his hands, caressed his pompadour, blew kisses. "It's the only amusement they get, poor dears," he said," "aside from fucking each other at night."

The jail overlook was on my route now, but when I got there, I found the recreation yard empty. A boy told me the jail had been closed. There had been too many escapes. Now the prisoners went to La Dama Blanca, the big prison in Río Piedras.

I walked back to the hotel slowly, along Calle Cristo, which was lined with elegant shops and galleries. Madison Avenue, Caribbean style. My sense of futility returned. I was using up precious energies here, and for what? To track down a few violent fantasies of Sonny Barowski. Whatever Miles had been mixed up in, it was unlikely we would discover it. The trail was well camouflaged, and it was cold.

At lunch, Sonny had announced that last month they'd found twelve bodies in a 24-hour period. "*Jueves sangriente*," he'd announced, "bloody Thursday." I thought, watching him, that if he'd had a tail he would have wagged it.

§ § §

Marie Barowski met me at the door of their apartment.

She was wearing a muumuu – white frangipani blossoms on a wine background. It was very beautiful. She said she had made it herself. I could hear Sonny talking in the living room behind her.

Ocasio Flores was a thin, dark man with piercing blue-green eyes. He shook hands warmly. I looked around. Reginaldo at the AIDS Hotline was right – this was the most beautiful apartment in the old city. It had a sweeping view of the harbor, bay, docks, mountains. It was hard to turn away from it.

"Ocasio was telling us a story," Sonny said, with one of his grim smiles. "He just got back from Yabucoa. Tell Bruce."

Ocasio looked embarrassed. "I wrote the story for the newspaper. Very bad publicity."

"We all need to hear the truth," Sonny went on. He had a drink in one hand.

After some more prompting, Ocasio began. "An American company leased some *terreno* near Yabucoa, maybe a thousand hectares, to grow cantaloupes. Good earth, plenty of rain and sunshine. They expect to get two harvests, maybe three, every year." He paused, shifting uncomfortably. "The people of Yabucoa, you understand, are good, *buena gente*, but poor. No factories, no jobs, nothing but *los cupones*."

I knew about welfare coupons.

"So they see these big machines come and they wonder, who are these men? What does this mean to us, the *residentes* of Yabucoa? Then time passes and everybody watch the melons growing. Big, beautiful, like a woman with child." Sonny chuckled unpleasantly. I had a sudden picture of what was coming.

"Finally, the melons are ripe. I don't know how they organized it, but one morning the owners go in the field and every fruit is disappeared. Gone."

Sonny clapped his hands. "Every fucking cantaloupe! They picked them by moonlight, trucked them to Mayagüez and sold them on the street."

But Ocasio wasn't laughing. "This is terrible. There were television people today. Very bad publicity for years." He hunched forward. "It's because we are a colony of the United States. People lose their pride, their respect. If they see the chance, they do wrong."

"Ocasio is an *independentista*," Marie put in. She was sitting on a love seat by the window.

"All the best people are *independentistas*" Sonny added, "but that doesn't mean they're right."

Ocasio shot him an angry glance. I hoped we weren't going to get into an argument about the status of Puerto Rico. But Marie intervened. "I can't take another night of politics. I get it in the faculty room all afternoon."

There was a pause. I had the impression of gears being shifted. It was my turn. I wondered what Ocasio thought about *maricones*, if he shared the island prejudices. I had seen a *graffito* on my walk this afternoon, in English.

KILL A FAG A DAY
TO CHASE THE AIDS AWAY

I had averted my eyes but not in time.

I took a deep breath. "Sonny says you knew my friend Miles Halloran."

Ocasio smiled. "Everybody knew Miles."

"Is it true he was mixed up with some shady characters?"

Ocasio nodded. "I wrote a series on the vice on the island. A man named Tupi Rivera controls most of the girls. I went with *la jera* on a raid to Tupi's Club. They expected to find a few customers, some girls, make an arrest. Nothing big. But when we all went into Tupi's private office your friend Miles was sitting there. A tall, thin man, bad skin, hair the color of the burnt sugar sauce in a flan."

"That sounds like him."

"Never learned to speak Spanish?"

"He expected everyone to speak British English."

"El NIC, the police investigators, asked why he was there, he said he was putting up a painting. He was a painter, true?"

"He was all sorts of things. In fact, Sonny and Marie bought one of his paintings years ago." I looked around the room.

"It's in the bedroom," Marie offered.

"I talked to Miles in the office," Ocasio went on. "I ask if he knew what kind of business Tupi was in. He said he never asks his customers about personal affairs."

"Then what happened?"

"Afterward I go to the *precinto* on Calle Tanca to see what they are doing with Tupi. His lawyer won't come down in the middle of the night, so they lock up Tupi. He made a big noise."

"You could hear him across the city," Sonny observed.

"Next day," Ocasio went on. "I was writing my story and Luis Real, the man in charge of the investigation, called to ask how well did I know Miles Halloran. Also, was it true he was homosexual."

The word, with its dropped "H" was soft and sonorous in Spanish.

"I said probably. 'Then what he is doing at Tupi's Club is something else,' Luis said."

"Did the police ask Miles more questions the next

day?" I asked.

"They couldn't. He went flying to New York. Later they hear he is in Europe – Greece, I think." Ocasio sat back, spreading his hands. "Dead end. *Calle sin salida.*"

We all sat quietly for a few minutes. I could feel a catch in my chest – my old enemy, rale. At last I said, "How are we going to discover the real reason for Miles's presence in Tupi's club? Miles wasn't questioned. He's dead. And I doubt that we'll get anything out of Tupi."

"We have Eduardo Conde," Sonny said.

"Who?"

"Miles's good friend. He must have known what was going on. They were thick as thieves."

Marie broke in. "This whole thing is just so silly. Eduardo is very respected here. A good friend of Doña Felisa when she was mayor. He does decorating jobs at La Fortaleza. You've all been reading too many mysteries."

Sonny started to speak but she went on. "Even if Miles was mixed up in something, I'm sure it was small potatoes. All right, maybe he made some courier trips to Grand Cayman, but he wasn't the type to get mixed up in anything ... anything truly evil. He was simply too sweet."

"There we have a woman's intuition," Sonny observed.

I smiled at Marie. She had spoken my intuitions too.

"The fact remains that he was found dead in his New York apartment a few weeks after skipping out of Tupi's Club and Puerto Rico," Sonny said.

"Isn't New York the crime capital of the world?"

But Sonny cut her short. "Anyway, let's pay a call on Eduardo Conde tomorrow morning. What have we got to lose? And Bruce has come all this way."

Yes, all this way, to track down some vaguely paranoid suspicions by a frustrated crime reporter. And then

I understood what had brought Barowski to this particular outpost of expatriates. His phone calls to me proved it. Also his general bloodthirstiness and the gunshot wound in his leg. He had come to Puerto Rico to win his tin star.

8

I CALLED SCHOOL FIRST THING in the morning. Nothing disastrous, Erica told me, except that Fiona McCleary had a new request for our Christmas recital. She had discovered a Gottschalk piece for eight pianos. It would give all her advanced students a chance to shine. "Where are we supposed to get eight pianos?" I asked.

"I raised that question with Miss McCleary and she said it wasn't her responsibility."

"Maybe we can rent some Casios," I said. The thought of Fiona conducting eight students at electronic keyboards was pretty funny.

"She'd love that," Erica replied. "What do you want me to tell her?"

"Tell her no dice."

Erica asked about my activities on the island. "Miles had some strange friends here, but nothing the police would be interested in. No one who could replace David in that circumstantial net of theirs."

"Well, everyone here is terribly upset. I certainly hope something turns up." After ringing off, I went down to the patio for breakfast. It was deserted except for several waiters who served me papaya, *pan dulce* and rich Spanish coffee. Unfortunately my appetite, which had been playing hide-and-seek for the last few weeks, chose this morning to disappear completely. I crumbled a few bits of bread and sipped the coffee. The papaya slice I had to leave untouched.

After breakfast I went upstairs for my bathing suit. After our session with Eduardo Conde, I would ask Sonny to drop me off at the beach. Despite Dr. Zinsser's warning about the sun I had decided to risk it. And risk being seen almost nude – I'd lost about 15 pounds.

§ § §

The shop bell jangled as we went in. The man who came from the back of the shop was about my age, squarely built, olive-skinned, with a helmet of closely-cropped grey hair, rimless glasses. He had a tight, professional air. At first I thought I was face-to-face with your standard showroom queen, but Eduardo Conde was anything but that. In fact, he reminded me a bit of Reginaldo at the Hotline. He gave Sonny a warm *abrazo*, and took my hand in both of his when we were introduced. Immediately he ushered us back to his office and started making coffee. On the way, passing through the rooms of the shop, I noticed the usual wicker and rattan furniture, also chairs and sofas in rich tropical woods, upholstered pieces in bright fabrics, screens, tables, dining sets, and decorative objects. White painted wall sconces seemed to be a big item, also mirrors, bleached wood sculptures and some flashy lithographs, flamboyantly framed. It was a shop, I suspected, for the ostentatious and the well-to-do. But then I checked myself – decorating a home in the trop-ics wasn't a subject I knew anything about. There was no reason to pass judgment.

One item did stand out, however – a studio piano with a silken white finish. I ran my hand across the top, wondering about humidity and termites. And then something above it caught my eye. A familiar face – one of the *caballero* masks I had seen in New York. This one was staring white, with the gaping eye holes and turned-down mouth.

"My friend Miles Halloran used to bring in those masks," I said, catching up with Sonny and the proprietor in the back office.

"Oh, yes," Eduardo said, "he started a little business in that." He waved his hand. "Oh, many years ago. I help him a little bit at first. But then it was a success and he didn't need my help."

He busied himself with the coffee. "Miles did too many things. What do you call that in English?"

"Jack of all trades?"

"Yes, that's it." He repeated the phrase with satisfaction. "He paints a little, he dances a little, he writes a little, he does this and that. And finally he goes into the import business. And after that, something goes bad and he is dead."

While we waited for the coffee, Eduardo told us about his first meeting with Miles. Miles had walked into this shop with three or four of his paintings under his arm, wrapped in oilcloth. Eduardo put his wrist to his forehead in a dramatic gesture. "Oilcloth! I am positive this oilcloth Miles had been using since he was a schoolboy in England. He carries his books in it to protect against the rain. And here he is in Puerto Rico, maybe 50 years later, with the same oilcloth. Do you know what I think when I see that oilcloth? Here is either a genius or a crazy person."

I laughed. "Which was it?"

"To tell you the truth, a combination. The paintings are not very good, mostly trees, landscapes, boats, but each one has a little touch. A crazy touch. Purple and black for the trees. Chartreuse for the water. Little pieces of mirror pasted on for sunlight. I said, 'You can do more like these?' He told me he can paint whatever I want. Three, five a week. I set up a room just for Miles Halloran. I show you later."

Sonny turned toward me. "I told you Eduardo and Miles got to be friends."

"Oh yes." Eduardo touched his chest. "I love Miles. He is original. *Un original.* I take him to visit friends on St. Thomas, on St. John. They love him too. Every time he sends a painting as a thank-you gift."

The coffee was ready. It was Cuban, strong, with hot milk. "Then you probably know what Miles was doing at Tupi Rivera's club the night the police raided it," Sonny said. "That's the one thing we can't figure out."

"Oh!" Eduardo waved his hand, a dismissive motion. "I sent him there. I said, 'Tupi doesn't know where to put your painting, go over and hang it for him. The light is bad in Tupi's office, and the *flamboyán* tree looks dead.' And next thing the office is full of policemen and reporters. Miles was so frightened he left the island the next day." He paused. "I never saw him again."

I looked at Sonny, who looked uncomfortable. "So he wasn't working for Tupi?" Sonny asked.

Eduardo let out a bellow. "Miles and Tupi? You are making me laugh. Come, I show you."

He led us to a smaller room off the main showroom. It was a gallery. The walls were full of original oils but I had no trouble picking out those by Miles. There was something ... well, slightly bizarre about each one. A sailboat with a tiny Jolly Roger drooping from the mast. A farm with a bullwhip threaded into a stile fence. A tree with a pair of ballet slippers hanging from one branch.

"And you still sell them?" I asked.

"Oh, yes." The hand wave again. "Now I don't know what to do with the money, but I keep it. One day somebody will walk in and say, 'I am Miles Halloran's niece or cousin,' and then I give it all back."

A charming sketch, in pastels, caught my eye. A handsome stone house, bougainvillea falling from roof to porch, planters with Grecian edgings built into the stairs and porch. I looked at the lettering in the lower right comer, *Finca Vigía, Cojímar, 1940.* I started to ask about it but Sonny had a more important question.

"Miles was seen on Grand Cayman, at one of the banks in Georgetown, not long before he died. The rumor was that he was running drug money. Do you think that was true?"

Eduardo's cheery manner changed. "Yes, I heard that too." He shrugged. "But I think it was coincidence. He was there on vacation. You know Miles liked to travel. Anyway, I asked Tupi about it once. I designed the bar in his club, caoba wood, very fine, and had it built especially in Arecibo – and he always tell me the truth. He said he had no business with Miles except to buy that painting."

"Then how did Miles get the money to buy his new apartment in the Condado?" I asked.

Eduardo shrugged again. "I think one of his aunts in England died. He told me he was going back there for the funeral. So maybe ..." He trailed off. "That was two years ago."

Sonny was nodding unhappily. His theories were being torpedoed. More than that, his status as concocter of conspiracy was being destroyed.

We didn't stay long after that. Some customers arrived and Eduardo was called away. Sonny didn't say much as we made our way back to his Volvo, nor did I. The purpose of this trip was slowly seeping away. I began to think about calling the airline and going home.

Sonny might have read my thoughts. "I don't think you should leave until we've visited Tupi's Club."

"What are we going to find out there?"

"I don't know, but we might as well give it a try."

"When?"

"Tonight?"

I agreed reluctantly. The heat in the car was like a mailed fist. Just as we pulled away from the curb, a blue van veered sharply from the oncoming lane and made a left into the Casa Cristal driveway. The van carried the shop logo on its side. I caught a quick glimpse of the driver – another handsome New Tahitian, with a knob head, the usual mustache, and a pony tail. The next instant he had pulled out of sight.

§ § §

I was in luck. José Villalón and his American friend, Mike Freed, were at the beach. I saw them as soon as I stepped from the fringe of palms. I had met them through Miles years ago – José stocky and round-faced, in his early thirties, Mike blond and delicate. They didn't live together, merely met as José's busy schedule permitted. José phoned and Mike hopped a plane.

José was *Colombiano*, in the sneakers business. The Villalón family had factories in Miami, Santo Domingo, Caracas. There had been a factory in Cali, in their own country, but the drug cartel had made life impossible there. Now José, the son and heir, shuttled around the plants, customers, suppliers. He kept an apartment in Puerto Rico for relaxation. He had gone to school in Miami.

I felt a little uneasy as I stepped into the underbrush to change to my swimsuit. Would my body betray me? Send its own message? Suddenly I wanted this little visit to the beach, the beach that was Miles's favorite and my own, to be untarnished. To be as before. When I came back, José said the news about Miles had been in all the local papers, Spanish and English.

I kept the hotel towel draped across my shoulders. I also had a straw hat, bought from a vendor at the beach entrance. I sat down gingerly. They didn't seem to notice anything. I dug my toes into the sand; José did the same. His was a body type I didn't find attractive – round but hard, like a barrel. Things bounced off that body easily – off José's spirit too. The Villalón family, I had noticed before, had a vocation for the world. José began to talk about their trip to Haiti.

"We rented a car in Port-au-Prince and were on our way to Cap Haitien. Right across the island." He paused, shaded his eyes. The distant sound of bongos had reached him – the mating call of a stressed latino. But no one was within sight. "Anyway, we got to this village and they were crazy about Michael." José looked at his friend and grinned. "I don't think they see many blonds. Or maybe they thought he was a movie star. This old man comes up and offers to buy Michael. I'm not shitting you. We're in the middle of Haiti and we get an offer. I ask him how much. He takes us to his house, which is a tin shack, and says we can have anything there. There were a couple of chickens and goats and an old cow stepping on her tits. Michael started getting really nervous."

"Come on, José, I wasn't nervous at all."

"I asked the guy why they wanted to buy him but he wouldn't tell me. I figured they were going to eat him."

"Oh for God's sake, José." Michael turned to me. "They wanted me to help out with some kind of ceremony, probably. They were having a drought and they thought I could help."

José interrupted. "I said, sure you can have him, but it'll cost you a thousand dollars, you don't find an ass like that every day."

"He didn't say any such thing, Bruce. He gave the old guy twenty bucks in American money, which almost killed him, then we got back in the car."

I threw back my head. Crazy things were still happening in the West Indies. Magic was still alive. Why shouldn't I believe in its application to myself? And then, suddenly, it was impossible not to go in the water. I'd swum here dozens of times, all the way out to the crescent of limestone blocks that created the lagoon, and seen many marvels. Now, in a fit of normalcy, I borrowed José's snorkel. It was just like old times, though when I fitted the mouthpiece to my teeth I had a twinge of guilt. I shouldn't be mouthing his snorkel.

I didn't make it to the limestone reef. Halfway there I ran out of everything. I turned around, flopped back to shore and threw myself on the sand, mumbling something about being out of shape. José and Mike didn't say anything but the next instant, the hotel towel over my face, I was asleep.

Half an hour later I sat up. They were both smiling at me in a kind way.

My secret was out. José said that last week Cardinal Aponte gave a sermon in the Cathedral to say we all deserve to die: "It's God's punishment." Then he made an obscene sound. "But half the machos are still available, not just for money but for a good time."

After that I described my situation. There wasn't much they could say. They invited me back to their flat for lunch.

Twenty minutes later we were in the Saab, top down, rolling across the Dos Hermanos Bridge toward the Condado. Miles's last condo was on our route and when we reached it, José turned around. "You wanna go in? I got the key."

"You do?"

"I kept an eye on things when Miles wasn't here. He did the same for me."

Without waiting for an answer, he swerved into the parking area, pulling into a spot marked Cond. Staff Only.

"Isn't the apartment sealed, José? In New York the police spin a yellow tape around the scene. Nobody can cross it."

"This is Puerto Rico, man. The police don't do shit." He switched off the ignition.

Inside, at the elevators, a balding man in a matching cabana outfit surveyed us nervously. "*Buenos,*" José said politely. The man replied in Spanish. He got off at the third floor; we were going to the eighth. I recalled something Miles had said about gentlemen in cabana outfits: *Never* speak to them.

As we wandered around the apartment, where everything seemed in place, I asked José, "Why do you think he bought this?"

José shrugged. "Had some extra change, decided to get out of that hole on Sánchez." He paused. "He got tired of living in the gutter."

"Did he tell you where the money came from?"

"Never asked. Miles didn't like to talk about money, you know that."

"Eduardo Conde said he inherited something from an aunt in England. Do you think that's possible?"

Another shrug. "Could be."

I went into the bedroom. There were some photos on a bureau. I could see a man and woman with a boy aged seven or eight – a boy with Miles's quick smile, almond eyes. Another photo of Miles in front of St. Peter's, the Bernini arcade, in his 40s. I slid open a closet door and saw his shirt collection – multicolored plumage for a hundred different occasions. What would be done with these?

"Who are you? Who let you in?"

The voice was female and furious. It was coming from the other room.

She'd changed in the three years since we'd met – thinner, smaller, harder. Her freckles, probably cute at thirteen, had expanded into stains and blotches.

Her hair was a lifeless melange of ginger and grey, the result of too much salt air, too few touch-ups. "Hello, Jane," I said.

She didn't remember me. I had to introduce myself, and even then her greeting was grudging. She barely spared a glance for José and Mike, when I gave their names.

"This apartment is closed. It's supposed to be locked." She moved around the space in a proprietary way. And then I remembered. She was a real estate agent.

"Are you trying to sell this place?"

"I have certain responsibilities here," she said.

I knew the agency she worked for – West Indies Real Estate, the most aggressive outfit in the area. "Miles put this up for sale before his death? Signed the papers?"

She looked at me furiously. It was none of my business and she wanted me to know it. "What is your legal relation to Miles Halloran?" she asked.

"Friend. I came down here trying to pick up some clues on who killed him. Strictly personal. Amateur. Illegal."

That mollified her slightly. "Well, you won't find anything useful in this apartment. Probably not on the whole island. The criminal investigations here are pathetic."

"I've been discovering that." I paused. "Anyway, I'm glad Miles took care of some business things before he died. He wasn't your most – practical person." I looked around the apartment. "At least this'll be disposed of."

Suddenly she sank into one of the chairs. "It's not what you think," she said.

We all looked at her. She was really a tiny person.

"Miles went to Velez y Oquendo, the big legal firm, a few weeks before he left the island the last time. He donated this apartment to the Departamento de la Salud Pública stipulating that it be used as a hospice for sick people. I don't know where he got this bright idea, but he drew up the papers. The government people went along. He named me and two other friends to an executive board." She paused. "Of course, it's all a mess. There are no funds for maintenance. We have an apartment and no money to run it."

"Can't you raise the money?"

"That's what we're dealing with now. We're trying to get one of the pharmaceutical companies to back us." She clenched her small fists. "I've half a mind to walk out, forget the whole thing. But when Miles asked me to do it, I said yes, and I don't like to go back on my word."

It was my turn to sink into a chair. "So Miles wanted this ..." I gestured to the beautiful rooms, perched on the edge of the Atlantic, "... to be used for sick people."

"I suppose he had AIDS in mind, but he didn't say so.

It's probably better that way."

"But why do you think he did it?"

"Why? That's a good question. Frankly, I think he knew something was going to happen to him. He wanted to do one good deed." She fluttered her eyelids. "He lived a life of almost total self-indulgence."

I couldn't argue with that. At last I said, "I'll make a contribution. Give me your address and I'll send you a check when I get home."

She brightened at that. "Send it to West Indies Real Estate. I'm doing all this out of the office."

We talked a little more about Miles after that, but I could see she was impatient for us to leave. She didn't really want to be involved in motives and personalities. It wasn't her style.

We left her in possession. Going down in the elevator, I looked at her card. "Jane McTeague," I said to José.

"A bitch on wheels," he remarked.

After lunch at José's penthouse – a meal of palm hearts, cheese, chicken terrine, olives and *pain del pats*, all picked up at the corner deli, and which I had hardly been able to touch – they called me a radio taxi. They went downstairs with me, each giving me an *abrazo* in the Spanish style. I promised to call before leaving the island.

A hospice for the dying. I wondered if my situation had helped lead Miles to a last act of charity.

§ § §

Lust, almost forgotten, tip-toed into my dreams that afternoon. As I sank into the bed at El Convento, I felt vague sexual stirrings which burst into full flower once I was asleep. It was like greeting old friends, friends I

146

hadn't seen in months, whom I had missed. Gorgeous male bodies, thick with muscles, coming to a vital point between marvelous legs, grappling with me, consuming, devouring me. An enrichment that I needed desperately. When I woke up, exhausted and elated, I finished off the dream. I had been warned by several friends, and by my readings, that the libido is one of the first casualties in the AIDS wars, but I hadn't believed it when I heard it. How could that powerful force disappear? What would be left? But it was true.

I lay for a long time, gathering my forces, until around four I struggled up and into the shower.

I rested some more until hunger roused me. It was six. I might be able to tolerate an omelette and a flan. I knew where to go – El Jinete on Recinto Sur. Inside its dark, tiled interior I could imagine myself in a little bistro in Madrid.

I made my way slowly through the old town, past perfectly restored townhouses. I was headed toward the docks. I caught sight of radio towers and super-structures. In port were the Carla C, the Sun Princess, the Amerikanis – sea-going cities. No wonder my hotel was half-empty. The tourists floated in on these giant pleasure domes, visited the town for an afternoon of shopping, an evening of boozing, then departed at midnight.

I heard shrill voices behind me. A small troupe of girls, *colegianas*, in plaid skirts and yellow middy blouses, shepherded by a small, dark nun. They were headed for the ferry terminal. I watched them disappear, then turned. The sign, El Barrilito, just caught my eyes. I had wandered close to Tupi Rivera's club.

I hesitated, wondering what to do, when a blue van passed me, heading toward the club. The lettering on the side panel barely formed itself into meaning: Casa Cristal. I watched it make a right, proceeding past the club. These streets had no name.

I started walking up, away from the docks, toward the club. I made the same right turn that the van had, but there was no sign of it. I was in front of the entrance to El Barrilito – heavy wooden doors with brass fixtures, now locked. The next instant I heard a heavy car door slam. It seemed to come from behind the club. An alleyway, cobblestoned, skirted the side of the building. It was just wide enough for the van.

I walked slowly, keeping to the inner, building side. I didn't want any surprises. If only it were a little later, a little darker.

There was a brick archway notched into the side of the building. I stepped into it for a moment to catch my breath. Then I proceeded.

At the back of the club I saw a parking area and loading dock. The van was pulled up to it. The driver was working out of the open doors at the back of the van, piling cartons onto a handcart. I caught sight of a knob head, a mustache, a ponytail.

I scuttled back to my archway and waited. Then I went back. He was moving the cardboard cartons, piled on the handcart, up the slope of the loading dock. Another minute and he was inside the club. The back doors of the van were still open.

I moved quickly.

It was so dark inside the vehicle I almost couldn't read the labels on the remaining cartons. Then something came to my aid – some magical power that expanded my pupils – and I could see. The top carton in each stack was stencilled to Miles Halloran at his New York address. I flipped open one box. My fingers dug through balls of waste paper and found – nothing.

Three minutes later I was back at the docks. Some security men at Pier 3 were deep in conversation. They barely glanced at me. I was surprised. The noises in my head were deafening.

I hardly tasted the omelette at El Jinete when it was served up ten minutes later, but the espresso coffee was pungent and aromatic on my tongue.

What had I seen? A broken link in a chain that connected Casa Cristal, El Barrilito and Miles Halloran. But so what? There were no conclusions to be drawn. Miles had suppliers on the island for his imported junk – why wouldn't it be Casa Cristal, or for that matter, Tupi Rivera? There was nothing sinister here. Miles wasn't capable of it.

Back at the hotel, I called Barowski. "Something's going on," he said, satisfaction in his voice.

I expressed my reservations but he wasn't buying. "Are we on for a visit to the club tonight, Bruce?"

I begged off. I'd had enough excitement for one day. We'd do it tomorrow instead. He had a play to review, but would meet me at El Barrilito around ten.

I went to bed, my mind in a jumble, wishing I could locate the certitudes of sex again, but they were gone, probably for another six months.

I hailed a cab in front of the hotel the next evening. When I gave the driver the address – El Barrilito – a spiky little smile crept from under his mustache. I watched it in the mirror. "You like, I know better place. Not pay so much for the girls."

I thanked him and said I was just going to meet a friend. We didn't speak after that.

The club interior was huge. Tables well-spaced, some intimate corners with upholstered furniture, a dance floor cleared out in the middle. Along one wall a hand-some, curvy bar, of light wood, no doubt the one Eduardo Conde had had custom-made for the place. I took a seat and ordered, unwisely, a rum Collins. There were some young women at a table in a corner in flamenco outfits. There would be a floorshow later.

"You down here on vacation?"

It was a pinkish, overweight man on the next bar-stool but one. A woman just beyond, no doubt his wife.

"Sort of."

The woman leaned across. "We missed our cruise ship in Miami, our plane was late." She chuckled nervously. "But they were nice about it. They flew us here free and said we could pick up our boat tonight."

"My name is Chuck." A soft pink hand extended.

"And I'm Bonnie. We're so worried about our luggage. We checked it straight through from Boston to the ship."

Chuck winked at me. "She thinks it's still sitting on the dock in Miami."

"I've been wearing this outfit for three days," Bonnie continued. "Chuck, buy the man a drink, what did you say your name was?"

I tried to reassure them with happy luggage tales. "Oh, I'm so glad to hear that, Bruce." Bonnie let out a squeal. "Chuck didn't want to come, he said the boat's going to be a geriatric ward, but my sister took the Napolis last year and ..."

I began to dial out. They were actually in a state of mild panic. It struck me that they'd probably never been south of Malden. They had picked this club, they said, because it was near the docks. They might hear the toots when the Napolis came in.

Sonny pulled up about ten minutes later. He inspected my new friends, then nodded toward a group of chairs in a corner. He was wearing a seersucker jacket and khaki pants. Also a string tie with a jade clip, in the western style. I said goodbye to Chuck and Bonnie.

As soon as we sat down I told him I'd made reservations for the morning. "I'd like to get this over with," I said.

He tried to persuade me to stay longer. Next thing he swung his jacket open and showed me a handgun held neatly in place by a little holster. I stared at it. "That's what I used on the kid that was climbing our *reja* in Trujillo Alto," he said, smacking his lips. I wondered what the kid had used on him the next day, but didn't ask.

"Don't worry, Bruce." He patted my knees. "I have a permit. Besides, the police here are my friends."

I started to ask why we didn't have a little official protection tonight, if they were such friends, but checked myself. I took out my handkerchief and wiped sweat off my face. This place was frostily air-conditioned but I was on fire.

A door behind us – a door I hadn't noticed, but which Sonny undoubtedly had – opened. It was marked *Privado*. A heavy, dark man in a flowered shirt appeared, followed by a slender, handsome man in a tan polyester suit. They shook hands. The heavy man moved off. Sonny stood up.

"I'm Sonny Barowski from the San Juan *Star*," he said in a mild voice. He put out his hand.

The man in the suit nodded politely. "It's a pleasure," he said, taking his hand. I was introduced.

"I wonder if we might talk, if you have a few minutes."

Dark, unreadable eyes scurried over us. I had the feeling that Tupi wasn't your average thug. "If you are here about the indictment, it is better to talk to my lawyer, Don Jaime Velasco."

"No, actually it's about a friend of ours. Miles Halloran. Dr. Pittman here came down to meet some people who knew Miles."

A measured nod. Then he gestured toward the door. We got up, leaving our drinks behind. On the way I thought of Sonny's gun. The bulge behind the flimsy seersucker jacket seemed very obvious. I suspected that Tupi had noticed it too.

The inner office was paneled in a dark wood. The main piece was a large, handsome desk. Behind it, facing us, was a painting of a *flamboyán* tree. It was well lit and glowed against the dark paneling. I didn't bother looking for the artist's signature.

Tupi sat behind the desk and offered us drinks. I declined; Barowski accepted a Scotch. Tupi stood up to mix it, moving gracefully. Then he looked at me. "Your friend Miles was a friend of mine too. I was sorry to hear what happened. He was *simpático*."

Sonny leaned forward. "We've been told that he had some business dealings with you. Some kind of work he was doing. Is that true?"

Tupi sat back, smiling. "Yes, we were discussing some things. Miles wanted to open a gallery. He needed some help with it. We were talking about it."

I glanced at Barowski. He was blinking hard.

"Not the usual type of gallery," Tupi went on, "where the local artists, they bring the pictures, you sell maybe one a day, maybe one a week. This was a gallery on – wheels." He smiled, revealing square white teeth, like Chiclets. "We take the gallery to the cruise ships when they come in. I am friends with the ship companies. They don't let the local merchants sell to the passengers on the ship, but maybe they make an exception for us." He smiled again.

"So Miles was thinking of going into – partnership

with you." Barowski couldn't keep the skepticism out of his voice.

"Exactly."

"Unfortunately he was murdered before you could work out the details."

Tupi spread his hands and shrugged. "That is the bad luck."

"Miles was here the night of a police raid," I said, "is that what he was doing – talking about a gallery? Eduardo Conde said he was here to adjust the hanging of his painting."

"Ah!" Another shrug. "First he fix the picture, then we talk."

I had the feeling we had reached another dead end. *Calle sin salida.* I looked at Sonny.

"I wonder," Sonny said, "if you'd let us look around your club."

If Tupi was surprised he didn't show it. "Of course. You are my guests. My house is your house."

Still, nobody moved. I sensed that a skin had been shed – a skin of politeness or forbearance. Sonny had a fixed grin on his face. I thought briefly of showdowns in corrals. Then Tupi stood up. "Come with me, please."

He took us to the kitchen first – a long, dim room with a couple of men and women working. Then he led us through some dark passageways to storerooms filled with cartons. I figured they were liquor and beer con-signments, soft drinks, food supplies. Walking behind Tupi, I had the unpleasant sensation of trespassing. And yet he was perfectly polite.

When we came out of the last storeroom, and into the corridor that led back to his office, Barowski was gone. Tupi stopped, cursing in Spanish. Not a sign of him. My heart sank. I might have known.

Tupi went quickly into his office, motioning me to remain where I was. I heard the click of a phone, some murmured instructions in Spanish. I stood frozen in guilt and embarrassment. *What was I doing here?* Tupi came back, showing no visible sign of stress and led me back to the main room. I could see my friends Bonnie and Chuck still at the bar. They waved.

The next instant the gunshot sounded. Just a pop, from the region we had left, but I didn't wait. I followed Tupi through the door marked *Privado*. This time we kept going until we reached the back loading dock. Sonny Barowski was lying on the paved floor, clutching his leg. His good leg. I could see blood coming from the calf. The heavy-set man in the flowered shirt was standing over him. Sonny had his gun in his hand, but the heavy man appeared to be unarmed.

"Look like our friend from the newspaper shot himself," Tupi said.

"What happened, Sonny?" I asked.

"The sonuvabitch shot me." He waved at the man.

"That is impossible," Tupi said, showing his Chiclet teeth. "My employees do not carry guns."

The next instant the discussion was academic because Sonny went into a spasm of jerking and kicking and then passed out.

"Please come inside," Tupi said, still smiling, "and we will call the police."

I kneeled down to Sonny. His pale skin was almost blue and his pulse was faint. It was time for mouth-to-mouth respiration but I restrained myself. No use adding to the hazards.

"I'll stay here until you call a doctor," I said. "And I think you better call his wife too. She lives at ..."

Tupi interrupted. "I know where she lives."

The shoot-out at the Club Barrilito was over.

ST. VINCENT'S, THIS TIME AROUND, was another place. I was sick. My bed was next to a window and I could look north to midtown but I didn't. I was concentrating on my inner landscape, most especially my breathing.

It had started the day after I got back from Puerto Rico. Dressing for school, I could feel my lungs slowing down. I did a few arm waves, deep knee-bends, tried some pulmonary sprays, but they didn't help. At last, walking to school very fast, I found some breathable air. But it didn't last. I was clogged up again by eleven. My house of breath was collapsing. Erica had been popping in and out all morning, watching me. At last she said, "Bruce, I think we better get you to a doctor."

"Never mind the doctor," I croaked, "get me to St. Vincent's."

She packed me into a cab and Luddie came along. In twenty minutes I was undressed and lying in a curtained-off partition in the ER. I had an oxygen mask over my nose and mouth. I tried not to think of Tim Currier in Roosevelt Hospital, but it was like not thinking about pink elephants.

The resident who oversaw this was a thin, blond young man who exuded no sympathy. I took an immediate dislike to him. Even in my distressed state I recalled what Queen Victoria had said of Wagner: "A clever but not a pleasing face." It struck me that my illness had not passed muster with him.

It was better upstairs, where they conveyed me and my mask and the cylinder of oxygen a day later. I had been dripped full of drugs by then, Zinsser had visited, and I felt a little better. I hadn't been able to eat. The diagnosis was PCP again.

There were visitors upstairs in the Coleman wing, of course, but I didn't have the lung power to talk yet. By that time I'd been able to sort out Puerto Rico, especially the nightmarish last two days, but I didn't try to explain to anyone. How could I? They wouldn't have believed it anyway.

Sonny did turn out to have good friends on the police force, but there were no witnesses to what had happened between him and Victor Martínez, Tupi's overweight bouncer. In the trial, it would be Sonny's word against Victor's. After I had made my depositions, affidavits, and posted a small bond to ensure my appearance at the upcoming trial, I was permitted to leave the island. Sonny's wound was not serious – it would not disable him further. He had passed out, I decided at last, not from loss of blood but from sheer frustration. He had found nothing by poking around the back platform of the club, and he had been slow on the draw. Way too slow.

As for the rest of it, our sleuthing of the killing of Miles Halloran – what had we discovered? Not much. Stories that overlapped or contradicted each other or meant nothing. Miles, it was apparent to me now, was a masterful manipulator of people. He got what he wanted out of Eduardo Conde, Jane McTeague, José Villalón, Tupi Rivera – and, for that matter, out of Sonny and myself. He had been doing it successfully for years, until it failed altogether. The trip to Puerto Rico had been a fiasco on every count – for Miles, for Sonny, and for myself.

Only David Donnenfeld was in fairly decent shape, although his experience in the Tombs had left its mark, as he had told me over the phone. Now, in my hospital room, he filled me in.

"You won't believe it, Bruce, they put me in a holding cell the size of a phone booth. They were required to get me to a judge for arraignment within 24 hours, but it took them almost twice that long and nobody apologized. Whenever I went in for interrogation they kept asking me the same questions over and over. Where did you get that letter that threatened Miles with death? What was your relationship with him? Was it true he financed your education and that you owed him a huge sum of money?"

I told David now about my inadvertent mention of this to Kerrison. He looked at me furiously for a long moment, then shook his head sadly. It struck me that the David Donnenfeld of a few weeks ago had disappeared entirely.

"You know what kept me from going crazy?" he continued, on another visit. "I played the Chopin etudes in my head. The chromatic, the double-thirds, the harp, the butterfly, the octaves, all of them." A bitter laugh. "A few more hours and I would have run out of repertory."

I thought of Talleyrand and his pins, my own copying of piano scores with a French curve. We all had our methods for dealing with imprisonment.

"After they heard my story about ten times they finally took me to Central Booking. They took photos, fingerprints, kept telling me the rap sheets had to be in shape and the more I complained the longer I'd be there. Finally, next afternoon, about 40 hours after they arrested me, they took me to the general holding pen. You can't imagine it, Bruce."

I decided not to try.

After some more time, Clay had turned up with Jim Slade to argue the probable cause affidavit. It hadn't held up. The judge had warned the D.A. he'd have to come up with something better. So David was turned loose. But just before he left, when they were returning his belt and shoelaces and valuables, Kerrison had stopped by. "The investigation isn't over, pal," he had said.

So I had been of no use to David, despite all my heroics. Less than no use. Not only had I failed to be here for moral support, I had run down my health some more. I started to explain, apologize, but David stopped me. "You went to Puerto Rico with good intentions, Bruce, don't blame yourself."

After about a week my breathing returned to normal. They removed some of the tubes going into my nostrils and arms. There was also a steady procession of people full of false cheer. Not only some of our school faculty, but Angela, Clay, Rita Osterkamp and a half dozen others. After telling me I looked great, they all seemed stricken, and I grasped the fact that it's the patient's duty to reassure visitors that all is well. It was an exhausting procedure, but most of them went away looking better.

Oddly enough, I kept expecting Miles to turn up in my room. This was a mnemonic trick, of course – a replay of his last visit, under similar circumstances in this very hospital – but perhaps it was something more. I was angry at him. More than that, really pissed. I'd gone on a wild goose chase, 3000 miles for Miles, and nothing had come of it. I wanted to let him know.

By the middle of the second week I was restless and out of sorts, despite the little TV that swung over my bed, my music tapes, the books and magazines people had brought. I was off all the life-support systems now, taking my drugs orally, and wandering around the floor to compare notes with other patients. Some of them wanted to talk about AIDS, some didn't, and a few, I suspected, would have been grateful for a hand-job. I didn't oblige, though I was tempted once or twice.

The camaraderie on that floor was a vital force. It was as if we had all joined forces against a mighty antagonist. It was hard to believe the cheerfulness I encountered, none of it forced. I think it was the first truly social connection some of these people had made in years. Lesions, fungi, tumors, fading eyesight, herpes, bleeding intestines, exploded lungs – *now they all had something in common.* Isolation was a killer, too.

And then one afternoon, just before dusk, Miles arrived. I was lying quietly, thinking about a conversation I'd had with a young Irish kid, whose doctor brother would have nothing to do with him, when Miles slithered in. It was the same hour he had visited before. I watched him slide into the same chair and cross his long legs. "I've come to tell you a story, Bruce dear," he whispered.

And then – part of the same hallucination – he started. The words seemed to go directly into my bloodstream. But of course, I had heard them before. It was the tale of the aged ballerina who trains a young man to partner her in the great roles. I listened without moving, hypnotized as always, even as I registered the time and place when I had first heard it. It was in Central Park, waiting for *Titus Andronicus* to begin, years ago. Now I listened clear through to the end. The ancient dancer, in a rage at losing her lover to a young American woman, burns down the mansion. At the end she can be seen on the roof, doing her leaps and arabesques until the flames obscure her and the house collapses.

When he finished I put out my hand but his chair was empty. The hallucination was over. My mind was through with its tricks. I was alone with my bottles and pills. And then a surge of healthfulness went through me and I saw it all with perfect clarity.

The video romance which I had taken home from the Harvard Club, based on a novel by Glinda Collins, had been borrowed or stolen from Miles. It was the same plot from start to finish, transposed from England to the south of France. There could be no doubt: somebody had arranged for the plagiarism. I had a pretty good idea who that somebody was. The question now, of course, was what to do about it. I didn't want to go on any more wild goose chases. The next one might do me in entirely.

Still, in the few days remaining of my hospital stay, the conviction of plagiarism grew stronger, as well as the knowledge that I would need more proof. What did I have besides an ancient, dreamlike recollection that could be easily discredited as the fantasy of an AIDS patient?

§ § §

Old Saybrook, in Connecticut, has its share of stately homes. I had explored this part of the state several summers ago, on a visit to the Goodspeed Opera. It was a land of perfect façades – stone walls, white steeples, sugar maples and center-hall colonials – behind which, no doubt, lurked the usual psychic terrors.

Polly Alvarado met me at the station, which was a tiny white barn. Two weeks had gone by since my discharge from St. Vincent's. I hadn't regained weight, which made me grateful for the crisp late fall weather. I was wearing two sweaters and a down parka. No one, not even Polly, would notice that, underneath, my bones were pressing hard against my skin.

Polly's house was not visible from the road, though several cats were curling in and around a stile fence. I glanced at her. She was dressed in tweeds, which gave her a bulky look. At the station she had given me one of her quick, piercing stares – the examination taught her by her doctor husband – but hadn't commented on my appearance. Then she asked me to call her Polly.

As we started up the walk toward a big one-story house painted barn-red and set on a fieldstone foundation, something caught my eye. It was the trees. The clumps of beech, birch, maple, had faces painted on them. I stopped to stare. At the juncture where limbs had been sawed off there were now eyes, mouths, teeth, ears, in all colors. At some of the joints there were clusters of little goblin faces.

Polly giggled. I noticed that when she was amused she clutched her left breast with her right hand. "I got the idea from Tchelitchew," she informed me. "You know that painting in the MoMA called 'Hide and Seek'? A little girl hiding under a tree full of faces? When I got home I decided to do it here. The neighbors would just hate it."

She giggled again and clutched her breast more fiercely.

"Did they?"

"Of course. They wanted to bring it up at a town meeting, but my lawyer put a stop to it." She paused. "There's entirely too much tree-worship around here. You'd think we were Druids. Come in."

The living room, at the back of the house, had a vast window with a view of salt marshes and beyond them

Long Island Sound.

"My husband loved that view," she advised me. Her voice was neutral but I heard pain underneath. "I've made an English tea for us, sort of a memorial to Miles. I'll just go light the kettle."

When she went off, I took the packet out and slipped it under a pillow of the sofa.

Polly came back with a Regency silver service which she set on the table in front of us. "In Athens, Miles warned me never to let tea steep more than three minutes. He was such a stickler, wasn't he?"

I nodded, then told her about the cup of instant powdered tea I had served him once. He had gotten up and poured it down the sink.

"How is your friend Glinda?" I began in a conversational tone.

"Betty Jean? I think she's working on a new book." She offered me a plate of crustless sandwiches. I could see a cake on the sideboard – the grand finale.

"A new book? She really turns them out, doesn't she?"

Polly shook her head. "I shouldn't gossip, but her husband left her a few years ago. She was at loose ends until she found this romance business."

"Her books sell extremely well, Clay told me. Especially the last one. What was it? *The Ghost Dancers of Rue.*"

"That was the next-to-last. The last was something about the jewels of Helen. You know – Schliemann and the excavations at Troy and the theft from the Berlin Museum and all that." Polly sighed. "Betty Jean has found a solution to the theft."

"She must be good at these plots."

"She doesn't seem to have much trouble."

I put down the cup of tea and leaned forward. "I want to tell you a true story, Polly, because I need your help. It's about Miles."

She looked startled. "You think I can help?"

"Yes. It starts, or ends, with Glinda Collins."

I began to spin my tale. How Miles had told me the story of the ghost dancers on an evening when we waited in line at the Shakespeare Festival; how I had taken home the video from the party; how I had finally screened it last week and found it to be a close replica of the original narrative. "And so," I finished, "I believe someone was stealing Miles's ideas. Someone who could profit."

She didn't reply, looking steadily into her cup. "You think Betty Jean is the one?"

"No." I shook my head emphatically. "I believe she has been fed plots by her editor. If so, she's the one who can tell us."

"And you want me to ask her?"

"You're the only one she might tell."

She studied her cup some more. "And what would you do if we ascertain that – the plots are not original?"

"I don't know. But we'd have a motive for his death. He might have been killed for his plots – as simple as that. They were quite valuable to some people."

She put down her cup and stood up. She wasn't pleased.

"You said when I first met you that if you could do anything to help with Miles, you would."

She moved around the room, observing her beautiful things. Finally she turned. "How, precisely, would I ask her? I can't accuse her outright."

I slid the packet from under the pillow. "Here's the video they gave me at the party. Screen it. Familiarize yourself with the plot. Then convince her that Miles told you the tale in Athens. At the Grande Bretagne. Or on the way to Aegina."

"But that was recent. This book was first published two years ago."

"Of course. He informed you it was an old story. He related it to you as a way of passing the time."

"That's not true."

"A white lie to get at what's really true."

She shrank into herself for a moment. Perhaps she was older than I thought – nearer 70 than 60. Then she straightened up. "You know, I run into Betty Jean at the local library every so often. It's quite good, actually. I remember, one day she was researching the south of France – poking over guidebooks. We left together and she talked about the vegetation and roads and climate and history of the area. Her backgrounds were meticulous. Maybe you didn't know that."

"We're not talking about background, we're talking about the spine of the story, the flesh and blood."

She went to the sideboard and fetched the cake. Very carefully she cut us each a piece. "I liked Miles very much but I don't want to get mixed up in this."

"I don't want you to get mixed up in it. I just want you to find out one thing."

"Betty Jean is very proud of her work. It's given her a great deal of self-confidence."

"We're not going to take that away from her, Polly. We're just going to find out a possible reason for Miles's murder."

A half hour later we were in her car, driving to the station. The afternoon had turned awkward. She hadn't agreed, she hadn't disagreed. At the station, after brushing my cheek and urging me to stay well, she said she would call me in a few days and let me know what she decided. When the train came in I climbed aboard with effort. I hoped Polly, on the platform, didn't see my stumbling.

Aboard, my spirits began to sink. The solution to the mystery, as I should have known all along, was in New York City. But unless Polly and her friend cooperated, there could be no proof. The pressure would continue on David Donnenfeld, who might not be so lucky next time around.

And then, in an unwelcome access of memory, I remembered some of Tim Currier's complaints in the months before he died. He had complained of mental confusion, inability to recollect, a tendency to drop things and a vague sense that he wasn't living his life any more. "Dementia," all his friends had thought, or murmured, nodding sagely at their diagnosis. Tim had had a CAT scan. When the results came back – Jim had said it was like passing through a giant bagel – his doctor had informed him, almost cheerfully, "No toxo, no PML lesions, no tumors, just the usual deterioration."

Just the usual deterioration. Was that happening to me now? Was this new thesis, the theft of Miles's work, just another sign that my mind wasn't working anymore?

We were almost to New Haven when my answer came from, of all people, Leslie Osterkamp. It was the morning she had asked about going for a degree at Pace. Her essay, the story of her life, had been written on her mother's computer, and there had been an accidental erasure. What was it? I forced my mind back, reconstructing the occasion. Something about characters with Russian names, some romantic nonsense. And then I found the words I wanted. *Her mother was furious because she had erased an outline for a plot.*

I had paid no attention at the time, of course – it meant nothing. Now it might confirm what I believed. Rita was obviously in the habit of preparing storylines for her writers. And there was no telling where she got them.

It was only a hint, a clue, and it might be explained away. But as the train creaked to a halt in New Haven, a vast easing went through me. There was no reason to doubt my sanity. I was on the right track.

10

"I **TRIED TO COMMIT SUICIDE.** If my friend Laura hadn't broken in, I wouldn't be here today. I woke up in the hospital."

The speaker was a bony, freckled man in his late thirties. "She thought I owed her something for saving me. Like I was in her debt. But I didn't. That's why she got sore. Nobody owes anybody a fucking thing in this business, you're on your own."

His voice was thick with anger. The rest of us – five men and two women – sat quietly, listening. It was my first group therapy session at an organization specializing in PWAs – People with AIDS. We were meeting in a church basement. I hadn't liked what I'd heard so far.

"That's not true, Charlie." A pleasant, dark-haired young man next to me spoke up. His name was Seth. "You can't do without help. Support. And you have to be grateful for it."

Charlie's face twisted – a handsome man turned hideous with anger.

"Fuck that. You're on your own, whether you got AIDS or not, and if you don't see that you're just kidding yourself. I didn't ask her to save me. And just because she did she got no claim on me."

I wondered what traumas lay behind Charlie's negation of human payback. A few minutes before, when I had first spoken, I had mentioned some old friends who had dropped me when they heard about my health. Charlie had broken into my recital. "What's wrong with dropping you? They got no obligation to look after you."

I could feel my brain heating up. "I don't want them to look after me. I've known a couple of them for fifteen or twenty years. We've been through a lot together. When I was in trouble they weren't there."

He glared at me. "Why should they be?" he asked.

I thought it might be time for Dorothy, our group leader, a maternal, sweet-faced lady and a professional therapist, to break in. But she was smiling benignly at Charlie and me. I could almost read her mind: *They're getting their feelings out.* The only trouble was, I didn't want to hear Charlie's feelings. Nor, quite honestly, was I keen to hear the other feelings in the room expressed. We were all in various stages of illness, weakened physically and psychologically. How could an hour and a half each week, trapped in a room together, alter those facts? More likely, we would turn our despair and rage on each other.

I couldn't help comparing this situation with the ease and openness of the AIDS floor at St. Vincent's. But of course there we were all down to the barest, meanest stratum of existence. We were dressed alike, treated alike, living alike. Social discrepancies had washed away, making us one. But here, in this church basement, with our individual attire, our solo histories, our burdens of selfhood, we had drawn apart.

Somebody else spoke up. He was a teacher at Parsons, not far from here.

"The dean, he says to me, 'We're going to keep you on, Joe, if you don't publicize your condition. That's the way it is, take it or leave it.'"

Joe looked around. "What do you think I should do?"

Advice was offered. None of it seemed very useful to me. Joe's dilemma had no easy solution. I glanced at my watch. Another half hour to go. Angela had persuaded me to sign up for these sessions, but Angela was into groups. She adored them.

I had been at school part-time this last week, the third after my release from the hospital. Everything had seemed extra-hard, though people were very considerate. There had been a loosening of ties, an unbinding. I didn't connect in the old way. I fought this, aware of my responsibilities, trying to re-inhabit my routines, but nothing quite worked. Detachment, perhaps a self-protective device, had built new walls between me and the school. I tried to explain this to Angela one evening, and of course she had the remedy.

"You have to join a support group," she announced, her round face glowing, "you've got everything bottled up."

"What am I supposed to tell a support group?"

"Everything you feel, naturally. You're not in this alone, you know."

Funny, I had the impression that alone was precisely where I was – alone with my lungs, my fatigue, my feverish nights, my long reviews of my life – but I let myself be persuaded. A group it would be. Angela made a couple of phone calls on the spot – we were in my apartment – and this Saturday afternoon was the immediate result.

"I haven't let this stop me one bit." The voice, from a tall man with prematurely grey hair, brought me out of my reverie. He hadn't spoken before. "Sixteen months ago they said I only had a few months to live. PML with all kinds of complications. I said to the doctor, 'I've got too much to do, I can't quit now.'" His voice was mild and pleasant.

He was an attorney, he said, practicing civil rights law. Some of his cases involved AIDS discrimination. "I moved my computer home and hooked up a modem, so I have access to my database at the office," he went on. "I can still make life miserable for some of those bureaucrats. They wheeled me into appellate session last week, a case I initiated two years ago, and I argued it even though I couldn't stand up to address the court."

A tremor swept around the room. Everyone waited.

"My eyes are affected but I bought myself a magnifying glass this big." He made a circle with his hands. "I can read anything, even the case law in my old books, which gave me headaches for years." He chuckled. I noticed that his eyes were unfocused, staring straight ahead. They were grey, like his mane. "I won that case last week." He chuckled again.

Suddenly everybody wanted to talk. Dorothy called for order, for one-at-a-time, but the enthusiasm was unstoppable. This defiance is what we came to hear, I thought, exactly this. Only Charlie was still grim. At last everyone had spoken and the session was over.

His name was Patrick Delaney. I went over to him when we broke up. He was a good six-three standing up. "I can take you home, Patrick," I said.

He turned his dim eyes on me. "That would be nice. What's your name again?"

"Bruce."

"I live in the Village, Bruce."

"So do I."

He held onto my arm as we left. He lived on Bank

Street, just a few blocks away from me, but four flights up. It took us a long time but he didn't complain. Upstairs, he showed me some of his things – not only the computer and printer but a FAX machine, a portable phone, a Canon copier. Everything was set up for independent living. I left my phone number and promised to pick him up next Saturday.

I walked home thinking I would call Angela and tell her what had happened. Not that she'd be surprised in the least.

§ § §

Polly Alvarado called that evening. It had been a week since my trip to Old Saybrook and I had more or less given up on her. But she had spoken to her friend Betty Jean after all.

"It wasn't easy, Bruce. I'm rarely at a loss for words but this time I was." She paused. "She said every single one of her plots came from Lightning Books. That's their name, isn't it?"

"Yes."

"They're developed in detail by the staff. Chapter by chapter. All she does is write it." Polly made a sound between a sigh and a laugh. "Of course, that's the hardest part."

"Did you tell her about Miles?"

"Just as we discussed. She was very surprised that the Rue story might have come from an outside source. Then she said she didn't care where it originated. It was a marvelous tale."

She paused. "It seems to me that even if there was some plagiarism going on, it's not a cause for murder. I mean, publishers don't *kill* for plots, do they? Even in these decadent times?"

"It depends on the publisher, Polly."

She wished me luck, expressed the hope that she hadn't harmed Betty Jean's career, and our conversation came to an end. I had the feeling it wouldn't be renewed. In fact, I had the feeling that a lot of things would be coming to an end if I persevered with my theory.

I went to the piano and tried to search out some answers in the harmonic certitudes of Mozart. Nothing there. Mozart had handled his demons in ways that were of no help to me.

§ § §

Clay suggested we meet at the Oak Room at the Plaza on Wednesday evening. Not a convenient place for me, but I agreed. He sounded cheerful about our getting together, which didn't make things any easier for me.

My new cane earned me some extra deference from the maître d' at the Oak Room. I had bought the old-fashioned kind, all wood, with a curved handle and diamond carvings going down one side. No tacky aluminum prosthesis for me.

When I lowered myself into the seat by the window, facing Clay, I was sweating but I felt mildly triumphant. I'd gotten this far. I'd be able to go all the way. David would be off the hook for good, no matter what the temporary cost.

He was halfway through a Scotch and I had my usual Perrier. The waiter, taking our order, addressed him by name.

After the opening amenities, I said, "David probably couldn't have gotten through the last few weeks without your help – the lawyer, the bond hearing, the general support."

"I wish he'd start playing the piano again," Clay observed, "it would make me feel a whole lot better."

I made some banal remarks about concentration and spiritual wholeness. The words slid off the table and bounced on the floor. We were both trapped in a third-rate script.

"I'm sure there'll be a break in the case soon," Clay went on. "Jim Slade is talking to one of the Human Rights Commissioners. If we can get it classified as a bias crime there might be more interest in solving it."

"My impression is that there wasn't much enthusiasm at the beginning and there's even less now. They just came down on David because he was nearby and appeared powerless."

Clay chuckled. "He didn't turn out to be so powerless."

"By the way, have you met the detective on the case? Kerrison?"

He nodded. "I saw him at the bail hearing. Big guy, freckles, looks like a side of corned beef?"

"That's the guy." I grinned.

It was time to switch the subject to Puerto Rico. I began to tell him about my trip, stressing the comic aspects. None of it seemed to surprise him. "We thought you were wasting your time, Bruce, but you were all fired up. Nothing could have stopped you."

I didn't recall that anyone but Luddie had tried to dissuade me at the time, but I didn't say so. "Anyway, it landed me back in the hospital, so I probably should have skipped it."

He nodded slightly. He was a man, I thought, who liked to be proved right.

"Except that I did find a couple of interesting things

at Miles's apartment in the Condado."

"His paintings, I expect. David said he had walls full of them."

"That, of course. I even found a gallery that keeps a full inventory of his stuff. But the most interesting thing I found were more of his famous shoe boxes. The ones he keeps his story ideas in."

"Is that right?" Clay barely stirred, but I saw a nerve quiver in his right cheek.

"He used to stash his plots in them in New York too. It's hard to believe, isn't it? Filing cabinets might never have been invented, let alone the computer. Anyway, he kept up his bad habits in Puerto Rico. Right next to his bed, in his new apartment in the Condado, I found one of the boxes, chock-full of 3X5 cards." I paused. "It's a pity there's no market for them."

"Did you bring them back with you?"

"Oh, I put a rubber band around them – there were only about a hundred cards – and stuck them in my bag. I guess I'll keep them as a memorial to Miles. You know, he used to tell me some of his stories. I always loved them."

Clay shifted position. "Yes, he liked to spin tales."

"On the other hand, I might junk them. My apartment is up to eye-level with memorabilia."

"I wouldn't do that, Bruce."

"Why not?"

"Well ... you never know. They might be worth a little something. One of the writer magazines might buy them. Some of those plot book companies might buy them. There are always writers with no ideas looking for material."

"Yes, I suppose there are."

A pause inserted itself. We looked out the window. The after-work crowds on Central Park South were hurrying home.

"Of course," he went on, "there are other markets for well-developed story lines. The film studios buy treatments. At least they used to. I could check it out for you."

"If I want to sell."

"Of course."

"Did you ever think that some of them might make good plots for video romances?"

"That market is pretty well saturated." His mouth turned down. "We should know."

"Don't tell me *Shadows of Desire* isn't doing well?"

"Not as well as we hoped." He chewed his lower lip. "But we've got some new marketing ideas that may help. A tie-in with a day-time soap for one thing."

"These things take time, don't they? I saw one of your tapes. *The Ghost Dancers of Rue.* Glinda Collins autographed it for me."

"How'd you like it?"

"I thought it was extremely well done."

He nodded in satisfaction. "We spared no expense. Sent a crew to the south of France, the whole works."

I waited for him to bring up Miles and the trove in Puerto Rico, wondering how he'd do it. It didn't take long. "Miles had some good ideas. He just didn't know how to execute them. Rita and I tried to teach him, even went in for line editing his novels, but it took too much time. We couldn't salvage his stuff. And of course he resisted our changes every inch of the way."

"Poor Miles. Even his paintings didn't sell well. Still, he must-have done well at something because he bought a fabulous place on the beach two years ago.

"So I heard. But wasn't he mixed up with some shady people down there?"

No shadier than the people here, I thought, but I held

my tongue. Clay glanced out the window again. When he turned back his face was smooth and mask-like. "I might be able to arrange for a purchase of some of Miles's stories. Assuming, of course, that they're halfway decent."

"What would you do with them?"

"I can think of several writers who might be interested."

"Not one of your stars?"

"I couldn't say. I might try them. If there's some interest, we could talk about terms." He waited a moment. "I assume Miles left no will."

"He arranged for his apartment on the beach to be used as a hospice, but aside from that I don't think there were enough assets to matter."

"Then there'd be no need to list these story ideas as part of his estate."

"You mean I could profit from Miles's work? Posthumously? From some material I swiped?"

"You can do whatever will ease your conscience, Bruce." His voice was deeper, authoritative. "Give the proceeds, if any, to charity. Donate it to AIDS work. There's nothing wrong with that."

He looked at me, his eyes dark and compelling. Now that the moment was here, that the trap had sprung, I found myself feeling guilty. I was embarrassed for Clay. I didn't really want to live in a world in which people could betray themselves so easily. It was as if an old promise to myself had been broken.

"You'd want to examine the material before you decide, Clay."

"Of course. You could bring it to my office. I'd like Rita to look at it too."

"I'd ... I'd rather do it at my place. Just the two of us."

Maybe he smelled trouble, because his nostrils

quivered. I could see wariness contending with greed. "When?"

"At your convenience."

"This is a pretty busy week for me."

At last we set a date for next Monday evening. He had never been to my place. I gave instructions. After that, we spoke of other things. He didn't want to dawdle, though. Soon he steered me through the maze of tables and slipped the doorman a bill to find me a cab.

Inside the vehicle, I settled back feeling polluted again. What had I proven except that Miles, in his cynical view of the world, was probably closer to the facts than I would ever be?

§ § §

The following Monday went extremely slowly. My nerves were on edge. That morning, waking at six, I had had a shock: I was dead. The realization occurred not in my mind, which was still registering impressions, but in the absolute abdication of my limbs. They were beyond command, beyond direction.

But the moment, scary as it was, was not without its compensation. I could rest. I could stop. And then, somehow, a button got pushed and the electricity started flowing again. But the body-memory stayed with me all day.

My last lesson was at three o'clock, an aspiring young songwriter named Martin Citrane who had decided classical harmony would be good for his pop career. His true interest was programming drum computers, but somebody had talked him into investigating melodic lines. Probably a mistake – he had a genuine talent for the speech of rhythm.

"What's this augmented sixth?" he asked today for the fourth time.

"Augmented sixth with a leading tone in the bass. Gives a nice resolution. Nice and fresh." I demonstrated. "Different from a V-I progression or a IV-I."

He diddled around for a while. "Art Tatum used that," he said.

"All the great stylists did. You have to make it your own."

But even as we worked, my mind was elsewhere. Clay would be at my place by six tonight. Everything had to be ready. We'd only have one chance.

I had brought Detective Kerrison aboard, for lack of better back-up material. I needed someone to run the audio lines, to tape the proceedings, and I didn't want to involve Luddie or Angela or Erica.

When I got home a little after five, Kerrison and his two sidekicks were busy. I found audio lines snaking from my living room to the back bedroom, and a couple of tiny mikes lying on the coffee table.

"Don't worry, Bruce," Kerrison informed me, "these'll be out of sight. We were a little late getting set up."

The two assistants – silent young men in denims with tool pouches clipped to either hip – taped the lines together, slid them under the rug connecting front room to back, and proceeded to tape the microphones in inconspicuous places. Shades of Abscam, I thought, looking around for the Camcorder. But they had decided against it. Sound would be enough.

The folder which I was to present to Clay sat on the coffee table. It was full of blank 3X5 cards. Nobody had bothered to fill them in.

"He's gonna want to examine this material before he makes a decision," I said to Kerrison.

"Stall him."

"Stall him? The whole idea was to ..."

"I know, pal, but nobody had time to write out a hundred complete episodes of *L.A. Law*, you know? Better if the folder is out of sight anyway. All we want is a statement that he wants to buy it. Oh yeah, make sure he's on that end of the couch when he talks."

I felt panic rising. Now that the time was here, the idiocy of the plan was getting to me. Clay would be way ahead of me, from the very beginning. What could I do but accuse him directly, tape his responses, and hope for something incriminating?

I watched Kerrison move smoothly around my apartment. He was a man at peace with his work, with himself. He had chosen intimidation and mendacity as a way of life, but it was new to me.

When, I wondered, had I started on that downward slope? When David gave his prime allegiance to Clay? When he was falsely accused? Did it go further back, to hopelessness over my health? Had I lost my bearings, my place in the world, when I accepted that sentence?

I thought back twenty years, to my time with Hector and Tim. Every morning, like clockwork, I headed downtown to teach at the Orchard Street Settlement School. A dead-end job that fulfilled me completely. What more could I ask than to waken those kids to music, give them a chance to make another world? The lousy pay, the long hours, the occasional frustration – none of that mattered. I was doing my work. There were no questions, only answers. I had finally solved the awful riddles of my childhood.

"I think we're all set." Kerrison, with his two sidekicks, came into the living room. "Joe and Kevin here can take off. I'll be in the back."

That was the way we had arranged it but a last doubt hit me. "Suppose he sees you back there?"

Kerrison shook his head. "He won't. Not if you do your job."

My job. Once it had been teaching beautiful kids how to play *The Happy Farmer.* I stuck the folder with the 3X5 cards in a drawer.

It was exactly six o'clock when the bell rang. Kerrison disappeared into the bedroom, pulling the door closed – almost. I touched the buzzer. The mikes and audio lines were invisible.

Clay was wearing a grey suit and carrying an attaché case. He looked around the living room carefully. "I'd say you're involved in music in some way;" He grinned. He was in a good mood.

I maneuvered him to the proper end of the couch. One of the little mikes was taped to the underside of the arm. "How about a drink?"

He peered at me. "You okay?"

"As a matter of fact, I'm not. Scotch?"

"That'll be fine."

I went into the kitchen, walking nervously, keeping an eye out. In the kitchen a coughing spasm hit me. I had to lean against the wall until it passed. Clay called out something helpful but I couldn't answer.

I came back with the drink. "You know, Bruce, if this is too stressful for you, why don't we just ... pass on it? It's not worth more health problems for you."

I nodded. It was a kind thought, but it came too late. I was locked into my downward slope. Nothing except total destruction would satisfy me. And I wasn't even sure why.

"Well," he settled back with his drink, "if you want to go ahead with this, let's have a look."

"The cards?"

He looked at me sharply. "That's what we're talking about, isn't it, Miles's cards?"

"Yeah." I didn't move. "But there's something else. I want to tell you first. It's a story, actually. One of Miles's."

He squirmed a little but didn't stop me.

"He told it to me in the hospital, a visit on the afternoon he died. I've been thinking about it. It's quite interesting. It concerns a man who was going to be murdered for his plots. He was a writer, very prolific, very successful. I can't remember his name but he lived in Hasbrouck Heights – a ridiculous place – and had a neighbor who wanted to get hold of his story files. The neighbor had mob connections and there was going to be some mayhem involved."

Clay stared at me, unblinking. "I was too full of Valium, too miserable, that afternoon, to make anything of it. But now I wonder if Miles wasn't hinting at something. Maybe even his own death."

Clay smiled easily. "You'll never get anywhere by trying to psych out Miles. He lived in a world that had almost no relation to the real one."

"I still think ..."

He raised one hand. "I'd like to get on with our discussion, Bruce."

The force of his will was like a blank wall. There were no cracks, no hand-holds. At last, giving in, I said, "I still have some ethical objections to selling Miles's stuff, Clay."

"I know you do." He made an impatient gesture. "You can ease your conscience in a thousand ways."

"You haven't set a figure yet."

"I told you, I have to see the material." He was getting antsy. He looked around the apartment, noticing the door to the bedroom for the first time. "Are we alone?"

he asked.

"Can you give me any general idea of what you'd be willing to pay?"

He stared at me, irritated. "A few thousand. That would depend."

I let his words decay in the lamplight. "That's interesting," I said at last, my voice casual, "because I believe you've been using Miles's plots for years. Plots like the one he developed for *The Ghost Dancers of Rue*. He told me that story long before either of us ever heard of Glinda Collins. And she's confirmed that you fed her the details."

"What's going on here, Bruce?" I had to admire him. He was in perfect control.

"Just what I told you. I have evidence that Miles's ideas have been plagiarized for years. Your willingness to buy more of them confirms that. I might add that there are no more. I made up that story just to see what you'd do."

Clay sat quietly. "What a fool you are, Bruce."

"Now the question is, were Miles's plots worth killing him for? Did the story files in his New York apartment add up to a motive for murder? As in the story he told me in the hospital? A search has been made and it looks like some of them, or most of them, are missing."

He looked at me ironically. "Is that what you're accusing me of? Coming back to Miles's apartment and hacking him to death?"

"Not you necessarily. Someone in your employ."

He guffawed. "One of my proofreaders maybe? What about Rita?" He sat forward, suddenly furious. "'You've made a mess of things, Bruce. First in Puerto Rico, now here. What about the death threats? Have you got those figured out too?"

"Yes. You wrote them to cover your tracks, using bad

English. By a screw-up, Miles gave one of them to David, which got him in trouble. That was the last thing you wanted to happen."

He laughed again. Just then the bedroom door opened and Kerrison stepped along the hallway. When he saw him Clay stood up. "So it's a set-up," he hissed. "I might have known."

Kerrison started to speak but Clay held up his hand. "Don't say a word. Don't read me my rights. I'll tell you exactly what happened." He sat down again.

Kerrison glanced at me then sank into a chair. Clay addressed both of us. "Miles was in deep trouble toward the end of his life, and someone killed him, but it wasn't me. He asked me to come that last night to help him. I didn't want to, didn't want to get involved. But David was coming for dinner and he persuaded me to drop by. When we were there, Miles showed us the two threatening letters he'd received. David foolishly took one home to study. The other stayed on that table."

"What kind of trouble was he in?" I asked.

"That's the ironic part. Ironic and typical. He wouldn't tell us. Just said he was in hot water and needed to disappear. He wanted my help to cover for him. Supply some income."

"And you agreed?"

"Not at first. The whole thing was too crazy. Like one of his gothic plots. Then he ... well, he made an offer I couldn't refuse." Clay turned toward me. "Rita had been buying story ideas from Miles for years. That's how we got *The Ghost Dancers*. Also a half dozen others. There was no theft, no plagiarism, but we didn't tell anyone. Not even our writers. It was all done by contract. And we paid him well." Clay paused. "But this time he offered his entire repertory, the whole kit and caboodle, all the stories he'd been cooking up since he was an adolescent. Most of them would be unusable, of course, but I figured ... well, I made a deal. Yes, I'd help him go underground, evade whoever was after him, feed him monies at stated intervals, in return for his files. He went in the backroom and got his cards, hundreds of them, and dumped them in a plastic sack. He said that tomorrow morning he was moving to the Langwell Hotel on 46th Street under an assumed name – Nigel Cameron – and I was to contact him there. His place would be vacated for good."

Clay set down his drink. The glass was empty.

"After the Langwell, he would move around the world. He preferred that kind of life anyway. He would set up some kind of itinerary for contacting him. But of course, he never made it out of his apartment. It was one last fantasy of his."

Clay turned to me. "I assure you he was alive when David and I left his apartment. We've been telling the truth to the police right along. And now," he nodded at Kerrison, "you've added a whole new element to the equation because you decided to play Miss Marple."

My stomach clenched like a vise. "Why didn't you go to the police yourself and tell them about Miles's plan to disappear? About the deal you struck?"

"Believe me, I wish I had. We'd done nothing wrong. But David persuaded me not to. He said admitting we'd walked out of here with some of Miles's intellectual property would lead to complications. It would be better to keep quiet. And the publicity, for our firm, if it got out, would be terrible."

I slumped back on the couch.

"That's the whole story?" Kerrison asked.

"That's the whole story."

He reached around and removed the little microphone from under the sofa arm. "I don't believe we've got any problem," he said. "Your pal David can back you up."

Clay's eyes went from the mike to me. "If you weren't so sick I'd smash your face," he said.

My mind went blank. I had reached the end of my own fantasies. I was so removed I hardly heard my front door open.

"Thank God you're still here." It was David, speaking to Clay, barely noticing Kerrison. "My apartment's been broken into," he said. "The door was jimmied open, the alarm disconnected."

Kerrison jumped up. "What was taken?"

"That's the funny thing. Nothing. Or almost nothing."

"What does that mean?"

"Just the stuff I was still holding for Miles. Stuff I was on the verge of throwing away."

Something came to life in me. "The masks, David?"

"Yeah. Those stupid plaster masks he imported from Puerto Rico. The carton he gave me not long before he died."

I WAS INSIDE A NAMELESS hospital. I saw grey machines, silver machines, machines on rubber wheels. I felt needles in my arms, tubes up my nose. The patients around me were pale and emaciated, a host of ghosts, some fighting their machines, others lying quietly. There was a terrible smell.

I struggled out of the dream. I could still feel the madness drifting through me. I had sweated ice floes, bonfires, through the sheet and onto the rubber mat. I found my electronic thermometer – 103°, a new high for a night sweat.

I lay there trying to deal with a number of ideas as my body cooled. Maybe the dream had been triggered by the long-delayed memorial service for Tim Currier. It had taken place yesterday, Sunday, almost a full week after our abortive drama at my apartment. After the service, which was held at St. Francis Xavier on 16th Street – a cavernous space festooned with icons of suffering – some of us had trooped down on the #1 train to Battery Park City with the ashes. It was a spot, at the foot of the esplanade along the Hudson, that Tim had noted. In fact, he had taken me several years ago while it was still being built, reciting a litany of unwanted facts about the site, architecture, inspiration. I half-listened, more thrilled with the estuarial sweep of the Hudson, the weird shape of the Erie-Lackawanna terminus across the water, the Statue of Liberty in the distance. We had walked past the slightly ersatz collection of townhouses and maisonettes, around a bend to a little bay. A gazebo stood next to the water. We sat down, peering out. "A great spot for scattering your ashes," Tim had remarked, pointing to the swift brown current. "In no time you'd be under the Verrazzano and out to sea."

I had shuddered at the time – it was an image I couldn't assimilate – but yesterday, with six or seven friends, we had stood at that very spot and taken turns emptying the packet into the water. When my turn came I recalled the rest of our conversation that afternoon. "Some bones burn more slowly, Bruce," Tim had said in his calm, well-ordered voice, "the skull, the sternum, the talus. They have to be raked from the ashes and crumbled by hand."

And suddenly, as I emptied out the bits of ash, the osteal fragments, I began to laugh. Timothy Currier, master of the irrelevant, had conquered everything – the winds, the tides, the past, the future, even his own death. He had done it by knowing. It wasn't everyone's solution but it was his.

After waking from my hospital dream I checked the time. Four a.m. An hour when the soul struggles hardest to escape its earthly prison. But mine hadn't succeeded this time. I got up and went into the living room, switching on the lights. My mind was active.

After David appeared at my door on Monday, telling us about the break-in, I relayed to Kerrison what I had learned in Puerto Rico. Clay and David listened with interest – David especially, since he hadn't paid much attention the first time.

"So what's the connection?" Kerrison asked finally.

"That's the question," I replied. "Miles imported masks, tourist junk, for someone on the island, then passed it on to some distributor in the Bronx."

"Can we get the name of the distributor?"

David shook his head. "Miles said to hold the stuff, he'd let me know what to do."

"I suggest we go over and take a look," Clay put in.

The three of them piled into Kerrison's unmarked Ford. I declined, pleading exhaustion. I didn't know what could be gained by an inspection of the premises anyway.

David called an hour later. "Kerrison's guys are here with white powder and black powder and little brushes," he said. "Also a miniature vacuum. I don't know what they're looking for, but the place is getting a good cleaning."

"Bits of hair, dirt, cloth, fiber," I said. "They'll take it all back to the police lab."

"Whoever it was didn't stay long enough to leave his signature," David replied. "Just picked up the carton and blew."

A thought struck me. "Tell me, David, what were the masks packed in?"

"Just waste paper balled up. Very careless. From what I could see lots of them were broken."

After hanging up I began to make a list. Miles had passed his carton of masks to David, claiming he had insufficient storage space in his apartment. Who knew about this transfer? There couldn't have been many. David and myself; Clay; Shirley Scott, who visited David regularly. Also some musician friends who probably hadn't known Miles. Was that all?

I went down the list again. David, Clay, Shirley, myself. A limited number with no link to the package, no business connection to Miles or Puerto Rico. I had drawn another blank. And then, unexpectedly, I remembered one more person.

Rita Osterkamp lived on West 18th Street, on one of those period streetscapes in Chelsea. The plate on the doorbell contained another name: Olivares. I wondered if she had a roommate.

She buzzed me in and I headed up a steep staircase which banked to the left. It felt unsafe, but Rita was at the door of the third floor rear apartment, watching my slow ascent with a warm smile. She hugged me. She took my cane without comment and hooked it to the front doorknob. Interesting odors permeated the apartment.

I looked around for Leslie. Rita read my mind. "Leslie moved in with some girls she met at your school – a flat in Park Slope." She looked pleased for a moment, then started on the dangers of living in Park Slope.

As she talked I looked around the apartment – my first visit. I was a little surprised at the decor. The furnishings were bright, almost garish, a cross between latino and oriental. Over the couch was a huge painting on tiles, vaguely art deco. It was called *The Judgment of Paris*, Rita informed me, and I could make out the goddesses and the apple, more or less. In one corner was a Coromandel screen, several dragons entwined on a dark field. A huge vase filled with pampas grass sat on a dining table. The couch upholstery was shot with gold threads and the two wing chairs opposite were mauve velvet with tassels dangling.

Rita saw me inspecting things. "Welcome to Miramar," she said. When I looked puzzled, she added, "That was the part of Havana my parents lived in. They brought almost everything with them, all their treasures. When my mother died and I had to clear out their house in Miami, I kept what I could." She laughed. "It's not my taste, but my mother went to see Castro in person and he let her take what she wanted. He could have put her in one of his camps instead – everything was on the dock when she was caught – but she persuaded him. My mother was very persuasive. So I felt I had an obligation."

I nodded. "When was that?"

"My parents came over in 1963, four years after Castro took power. I was six. I have almost no memory of the island."

A thought struck me. "The other name on your bell – Olivares. Is that your original family name?"

She nodded. "My father's name. I am Margarita Olivares Pereyra. My mother's name was Pereyra. Maria Pereyra de Olivares." She let out a giggle. "The Spanish way of joining wife to husband. It doesn't set well with the feminists. Maria Pereyra de Olivares means Maria Pereyra, belonging to Olivares."

"Then you're Margarita Olivares de Osterkamp," I said.

"I was until I got divorced," she said. "I should really drop the Osterkamp, but it's Leslie's name and I'm more or less identified that way in the profession."

Actually, I had known about Spanish nomenclature but had forgotten it. Hector Armendariz, my Dominican friend, had an extra appendage, just as Rita did – del Valle, his mother's name. I told Rita this, adding the story of Hector's appendicitis attack, which took him to Bellevue. Because of a mix-up, the name on his insurance card was his mother's – del Valle – which I had forgotten. I didn't locate him in the hospital for almost 24 hours. He had more or less been misfiled.

She laughed. "We know all about American dynasties, but of course you know nothing about ours. Olivares is actually a noble family in Spain. Velazquez painted the Conde de Olivares several times, mostly on his horse. He was a great patron of the arts. He helped Rubens, Murillo, Lope de Vega."

She spoke simply, her voice neutral, but she was obviously proud. "I know that painting of Olivares," I added, "or one of them. It's at the Hispanic Society. The horse looks like it's about to fly away."

She laughed. "There's another one in the Prado." She stood up. "But I have coffee ready." She looked at me. "You can drink coffee, can't you?"

I had given it up but I didn't say so.

She came back with a *café con leche* in a large breakfast cup and saucer. It was enough for three people. "Do you know, my father refused to drink coffee made by anyone but my mother?" She set the cup next to me. "It was like a fetish, even though there were other people to do it – myself, my brother, the maid. But my father insisted his coffee had to be prepared by his wife. It was a sign of love."

"I guess every family has its rituals."

She shook her head. "Only in Cuba is coffee so important. So symbolic. I'm sure it still is."

A few minutes later, we were at the dining table. She had made a bland brunch – ravioli and a small fruit salad. "Somebody told me you were eating mostly pasta these days," she said.

"I'm not eating much of anything," I replied.

It was good. I actually chewed and swallowed. After a while I asked her if she had heard about the break-in at David's apartment.

She sat back, her eyes widening. No, she had not.

I started to sketch the particulars but she interrupted. "I remember. David gave me one of the masks from that carton when we had dinner at Clay's that night. The night I met you."

"Do you still have it?"

She went to fetch the *caballero* face.

"I'm trying to figure out how many people knew this carton was stored at David's," I went on. "So far I can only come up with three or four people. Yet someone found out and swiped it."

She said nothing, just sat with the mask in her hands, staring into the empty eye sockets. "Who knew?" she asked finally.

"Besides David, there was Clay, me, Shirley Scott, you."

"That's all?"

"Well, David was out of town on his Central American tour most of the time the carton was there. That doesn't mean someone else didn't notice it. Or bump into it. It was right in the entryway."

She continued staring at the mask. I had the impression she was struggling to find something. "Miles was full of mysteries, wasn't he?" she said at last.

"His stock in trade," I replied. "We've solved most of them, but there are two that remain. Who wrote the death threats? And who wanted him dead?"

"Are you finished, Bruce?" She started clearing off. The questions lingered between us. "Did you meet any of his friends in Puerto Rico?" she called from the kitchen.

"A few. Nobody was much help. A lot of conflicting stories."

She came back with two saucers of flan. "This is for the digestion." She put one in front of me. The caramelized sugar gleamed milkily.

"Someone I met in Puerto Rico – a newspaper reporter – said Miles's hair was the color of flan sauce."

"Not a bad description." Her voice was neutral. I sensed she had taken a brief vacation from the conversation. I managed the flan, then asked for directions to the bathroom.

I was trying to avoid mirrors but this one occupied a whole wall and was lit up by bare bulbs. At first I closed my eyes, wishing for pink lampshades, but I had to look for the john. It was around a little bend. In passing, I saw an old man in the mirror. I looked away quickly but not before a reflected image, from the wall opposite, pressed itself upon my vision. It was a sketch of a handsome stone house, planters with Grecian edgings built into the stairs and porch, bougainvillea tumbling from roof to pavement. I turned and looked closely. It was a mounted xerox, in color.

I did my business and returned. Rita had transferred to one of the tasseled wing chairs, still holding the mask. I sat on the sofa opposite, under *The Judgment of Paris*. I would have to choose my words carefully, I knew, just as I knew that Margarita Olivares was in a trap as delicate as the one I was in myself.

"I noticed the drawing of a house in the bathroom just now. It looks like a beautiful place."

She smiled quickly. "That was our summer house in Cojímar. It had a tower room looking toward the sea. My father named it – *La finca vigía*, which means ... Oh, Lookout Farm, I guess. You know, he met Hemingway once, and when he told him the name of our house, Hemingway borrowed it, or stole it. For his place in San Francisco de Paula." She snapped her fingers. "But our house was the first *Finca vigía*."

"You said your father wouldn't let you make coffee, Rita."

"Oh yes." She laughed carelessly. "It's so neurotic I shouldn't have mentioned it."

"These things are always interesting. The inner workings of a family. He wouldn't let your brother Eduardo do it either?"

She cocked her head. "How did you know my brother was named Eduardo?"

"You mentioned him earlier, when you were talking about your family."

"I did?"

"Was he older than you?"

"Was and is. Six years. He was 12 when we left Cuba. He didn't really adjust to Miami. Said he didn't want to speak English all his life, he was going back to Cuba."

"Did he?"

"He did the next best thing. He moved to Puerto Rico."

I waited for an easy silence to collect around us again. Then I reached across and took the mask from her. Looking into its empty eyes, expressionless face, I asked, "Why did your brother take the name of Conde, Rita?"

She sat up quickly.

"I met him in Puerto Rico," I said. "He was a friend of Miles's. I visited his shop one morning."

Our eyes locked. "How did you know ...?" she began, but I interrupted her. "That he was your brother? I didn't until I saw the xerox in your bathroom. And even then I wasn't sure."

We continued staring. She shuddered briefly and I realized she had never intended to lie. "He wanted a studio name, something for his artwork, his sculpture." She passed her hand through her hair. "Since we're descended from the Count of Olivares, he thought it would be good publicity to call himself Conde."

"And when did he phone you, Rita?"

"We talk quite often."

"I mean, when did he call to ask for the location of the carton of masks that were shipped to Miles Halloran? The last carton?"

She stood up and began to move around the room, touching her mother's pieces as if they were magical in some way. "You mustn't think Eduardo is mixed up in this, Bruce. It's just coincidence."

"I just want to know when you gave him David Donnenfeld's address."

"Tuesday night."

"Two weeks ago?"

She nodded, then slipped back into the wing chair, burying her face in her hands. I ran my hand along the mask.

"Did he ask you the same question a few weeks earlier?"

She nodded, not looking up.

"And you told him Apartment 6E instead of 6A."

She nodded again. "There was a mix-up in the letters. E in Spanish sounds like A in English."

"Did you know that Apartment 6E was burglarized a few days after that?"

She looked up, finally. "No, I didn't." Again, I knew she was telling the truth.

"Would you believe me if I said your brother and Miles and Tupi Rivera perfected a way of smuggling crack cocaine into this country?"

"That isn't possible."

"I have proof."

She looked at me. I held up the mask. "It's right here, Rita. The face of a caballero. It makes a perfect item for shipment." She continued staring and I went on. "I've been doing some homework. If you boil cocaine hydrochloride with something called comeback plus baking soda, you can pour it into a mold. It will harden into a solid mass, just like this."

Her face was streaked with tears now. "If Eduardo was involved with this, Tupi Rivera forced him."

"Maybe so. But we'll have to let the police figure that out."

I don't know how long we sat there but eventually I got up, the mask under my arm, and headed for the door. I retrieved my cane from the knob. She didn't move as I left, nor as I closed the door behind me. On my way down the rickety stairs I tried to convince myself that it had all been worth it – the loss of the answers, the massing of new questions like storm-clouds overhead that would never dissolve.

12

THEY TOOK TURNS KEEPING ME company at home. Angela, David, Clay, Shirley. And from school, Luddie, Erica, even Fiona. Each morning around eleven, my front door would open – the key miraculously passed from hand to hand – and a familiar face would appear. During the first few weeks they made encouraging noises as they moved around. But gradually they realized I didn't need cheering up. I was at peace. Then they began to sit quietly, speaking only occasionally.

Of course, there were also good days when I got up, puttered around, played the piano, chased my visitor back to work or school. I enjoyed my solitude then; there were many ways to fill it.

One afternoon Detective Kerrison dropped by. I had taken the *caballero* mask to him the day after my meeting with Rita, and he had confirmed my theory two days later. The lab analysis had been swift. He had sounded a little miffed – how could he have missed such an obvious connection? – but at the end, grudgingly, he had congratulated me. "I guess two and two was staring us in the face, but you were the one who added it up," he said.

Then he asked how I did it.

"It was the packing," I replied, "or the lack of it."

"Come again."

"Somebody went to a lot of trouble to ship this stuff. If the masks had been valuable, they would have taken pains in the packing. Used styrofoam pellets or glass chips or cloth. But they used waste paper, the cheapest material available. Many of the masks arrived broken. In pieces. David mentioned this the first night I saw one of the masks – the night he gave one to Rita. But it didn't mean anything until he told me again, after the carton was stolen. Then it dawned on me. The masks had as much value broken as whole. That's when I added it up." I grinned. "Your two and two."

He went on to fill me in. Eduardo Olivares, aka Conde, had been arrested in his shop. Evidence was then found there – rubber face molds, some procedural chemicals, address stencils. Eduardo had fingered Tupi with only a minimum of police pressure. The cocaine hydrochloride had been supplied by Rivera, the mixing, molding, processing done at Eduardo's shop. The finished masks were delivered to the loading dock of El Barrilito for shipment to Miles in New York.

"Of course," I put in, "we don't know for sure that Miles was aware of the drug angle. He may have thought he was importing pure plaster."

Kerrison hooted. "He had to be making big dough. That's how he bought that apartment."

"Maybe they paid him just for receiving the goods, no questions asked. Plus payments for little favors, odds and ends, like going to Grand Cayman."

Kerrison shook his head. "He was going to make a killing. He separated this shipment so he could sell it himself."

"If that was so, why did he want to disappear? Start life over?"

"He was going to disappear for a while, then come back and claim the goods."

But something in me still resisted Miles's complicity. "Maybe he was involved with Tupi and Conde for a while. Maybe he profited and was able to buy the apartment. But he wanted to wipe that slate clean. That's why he set up the apartment as a hospice, to atone for his sins, so to speak."

Kerrison looked at me skeptically. "That still doesn't explain the boxes sitting in David's hallway."

"How do you know he wasn't going to notify the gang in Puerto Rico where it was, once he got away, once he became Nigel Cameron? Don't forget, his deal with Clay was for years of regular payments for his story files. Seems to me he was trying to get free of the drug profits and earn his keep legitimately."

Kerrison looked slightly stumped. "He was a pal of yours," he said at last, "you want him to look good."

I shook my head. "I don't think Miles ever decided whether he wanted to be a professional drug smuggler. And his hesitation, his doubt, did him in." I paused. "He was trapped in one of his stories and couldn't find the ending. Not a good ending where he could be a hero and keep a little of the loot at the same time."

We were silent for a while. "Did you find out who did the killing?"

Kerrison nodded. "Kid worked for Conde. His driver, I think. Conde himself wrote the letters."

I recalled the knob head, the ponytail. "He came to New York?"

"With his machete. Halloran opened the door to him. Stupidest thing he ever did."

Kerrison didn't stay long after that. At the door he put out a heavy hand. "You take care of yourself, Bruce." I promised. After he left, I realized I had never learned his first name.

§ § §

"Two, four, six, eight, AIDS does not discriminate!"

We were moving down lower Broadway, a wide phalanx of men and women, a few of us in wheelchairs leading the way. Patrick Delaney, of my group therapy sessions, was wheeling right next to me. He had called me about the action yesterday morning, asked if I'd like to participate. My first reaction had been – impossible – but after talking for a while he had made it seem possible. David was pushing my chair; one of Patrick's friends was pushing his. We were headed for City Hall. Traffic behind us was blocked all the way to Canal, maybe farther.

"Find the money, find the cure, anything else is horse manure!"

The chants rose and fell. It was five o'clock, people were leaving work, pausing long enough to note the tattered brigade rolling past. Cops on scooters were trying to edge us to the right, against the curb, without forcing a confrontation.

Suddenly there was a disturbance behind us. The line stopped. One of our own had been arrested.

"What's the charge, what's the charge?" An ACT UP lawyer, in jacket and tie, was yelling at a police captain. I didn't hear the reply but it wasn't satisfactory. The lawyer turned toward the rest of us. "Lie down. Right here."

Around me human figures scattered onto the pavement. David slid me out of the chair and then down. He settled alongside, his head next to mine.

"I never thought I'd be lying on my back in the middle of Broadway," he whispered. "I hope we don't get run over."

I was enormously excited. "I haven't seen the buildings from this angle before. They're beautiful."

Patrick was lying on the other side of us. He blinked his dim grey eyes. I didn't know how much he could see. "It's always the angle," he said, laughing. "Find a different angle and you've won your case."

A few minutes later the dispute was settled. I was back in my wheelchair and we were rolling downtown again. At City Hall, we demonstrated in a circle, just outside the police barricades. A woman, well dressed, came up to us and started digging in her purse. "I want to give you people something," she said. At last she found a bill and pressed it on David, who looked non-plussed. *Impulse.* I thought, impulse is the start of everything good. It was impulse that had led David Donnenfeld to the Longacre Music School, that had led to his first audition, to my taking him as a student. If any of us had stopped and thought too long, none of it would have happened. And that included the woman who wanted to do something for AIDS, or ACT UP.

"It's a free hair coupon!" David had been reading the imitation bill the woman gave us. "We get a shampoo and a styling at Joshua's Unisex on Park Row!" He let out a howl and showed it to Patrick.

The demonstration had begun to peter out. The point had been made – in this case, more housing for people with AIDS. A couple of TV crews had showed up, making the action a success.

We had trouble finding a taxi willing to load a folded-up wheelchair, but finally we did. Patrick and his friend had decided to stay downtown for dinner.

"Well, did you enjoy that?" David leaned over me in the cab.

I nodded. "It was marvelous." Things were whirling around. I closed my eyes.

I felt his breath on my cheek. "You okay?"

I had never felt so tired. The fatigue had scooped out a giant part of me.

At last I managed to speak. "Will you play for me when we get home?"

I heard a chuckle. I opened my eyes. "What do you want me to play, Bruce?"

It was a tired routine but we were still devoted to it. "Whatever you like, David." His hand, warm and fretful with life, closed over mine. Something flamed in the air between us.

We didn't speak much after that. The taxi, weaving through traffic, required all our attention. Besides, I had no further requests. I was already beginning to hear the music he would play for me tonight, and all the other nights I would ask for it.

RICHARD HALL

Richard Hall was a novelist, an acclaimed short-story writer, and a widely produced playwright. He was book editor of *The Advocate* from 1976 to 1982 and the first openly gay critic to be elected to the National Book Critics Circle. His landmark essay, "Gay Fiction Comes Home," was the front-page article in *The New York Times Book Review* in June 1988, and his reviews have also appeared in *The New Republic,* the *San Francisco Chronicle*, and *The Village Voice.* His debut novel, *The Butterscotch Prince*, appeared in 1975. His final two books, *Family Fictions: A Novel* and a collection of short stories, *Fidelities*, were published by Penguin. *The Spinner of Tales* was published posthumously by ReQueered Tales in 2023. Richard Hall died of AIDS-related complications in October 1992.

About ReQueered Tales

In the heady days of the late 1960s, when young people in many western countries were in the streets protesting for a new, more inclusive world, some of us were in libraries, coffee shops, communes, retreats, bedrooms and dens plotting something even more startling: literature – highbrow and pulp – for an explicitly gay audience. Specifically, we were craving to see our gay lives – in the closet, in the open, in bars, in dire straits and in love – reflected in mystery stories, sci-fi and mainstream fiction. Hercule Poirot, that engaging effete Belgian creation of Agatha Christie might have been gay ... Sherlock Holmes, to all intents and purposes, was one woman shy of gay ... but where were the genuine gay sleuths, where the reader need not read between the lines?

Beginning with Victor J Banis's "Man from C.A.M.P." pulps in the mid-60s – riotous romps spoofing the craze for James Bond spies – readers were suddenly being offered George Baxt's Pharoah Love, a black gay New York City detective, and a real turning point in Joseph Hansen's gay California insurance investigator, Dave Brandstetter, whose world weary Raymond Chandleresque adventures sold strongly and have never been out of print.

Over the next three decades, gay storytelling grew strongly in niche and mainstream publishing ventures. Even with the huge public crisis – as AIDS descended on the gay community beginning in the early 1980s – gay fiction flourished. Stonewall Inn, Alyson Publications, and others nurtured authors and readers ... until mainstream success seemed to come to a halt. While Lambda Literary Foundation had started to recognize work in annual awards about 1990, mainstream publishers began to have cold feet. And then, with the rise of e-books in the new millennium which enabled a new self-publishing industry ... there was both an avalanche of new talent coming to market and burying of print authors who did not cross the divide.

The result?

Perhaps forty years of gay fiction – and notably gay and lesbian mystery, detective and suspense fiction – has been teetering on the brink of obscurity. Orphaned works, orphaned authors, many living and some having passed away – with no one to make the case for their creations to be returned to print (and e-print!). General fiction and non-fiction works embracing gay lives, widely celebrated upon original release, also languished as mainstream publishers shifted their focus.

Until now. That is the mission of ReQueered Tales: to keep in circulation this treasure trove of fantastic fiction. In an era of ebooks, everything of value ought to be accessible. For a new generation of readers, these mystery tales, and works of general fiction, are full of insights into the gay world of the 1960s, '70s, '80s and '90s. For those of us who lived through the period, they are a delightful reminder of our youth and reflect some of our own struggles in growing up gay in those heady times.

We are honored, here at ReQueered Tales, to be custodians shepherding back into circulation some of the best gay and lesbian fiction writing and hope to bring many volumes to the public, in modestly priced, accessible editions, worldwide, over the coming years.

So please join us on this adventure of discovery and rediscovery of the rich talents of writers of recent years as the PIs, cops and amateur sleuths battle forces of evil with fierceness, humor and sometimes a pinch of love.

The ReQueered Tales Team

Justene Adamec • Alexander Inglis • Matt Lubbers-Moore

More from ReQueered Tales

Fidelities: A Book of Stories
Richard Hall

The *Los Angeles Times* says "Richard Hall's prose displays a rare polish, and his accounts of ordinary and exceptional lives unfold in graceful cadences." *Fidelities* is a stunning collection of stories that explores the varieties of gay experience – love stories, both passionate and compassionate; tales of suspense; narratives on the theme of AIDS; even a ghost story. Among the most adept and technically accomplished writers of his generation, Hall's third and last collection of short stories is an eloquent work of immense power.

Hall's short stories give a sense of having been distilled and polished over time till they glow with depth and wisdom. "Diamonds Are Forever" highlights a gay man and his married sister who are incapable of seeing shared traits that make it so difficult for them to accept each other; the story's carefully paced wrangling over an heirloom is masterful. "Avery Milbanke Day" features a 70-year-old writer – his seven novels about "the literature of hesitation" long neglected – decides to stay with his old dying lover and nurse him through a final crisis instead of attending a public celebration of his novels and himself. The "Country People" presents a gentle, eerie metaphor for the search for a sense of history, reflecting on previous generations of gay men and lesbians.

"Hall's stories evoke comparison with Henry James or Maupassant, Hemingway and Fitzgerald ... A luminous collection ... Hall has found in gay life stories to amuse, entertain, and move." — *Lambda Book Report*

Hall's final publication before his death at age 66 from AIDS-related causes, this 30th year anniversary edition celebrates his art at its peak. This new edition includes a foreword by Alexander Inglis.

The Butterscotch Prince
Richard Hall

The white marquee outside said Adult Films Only. Cord McGreevy, on the heels of a talkathon with his shrink, needed some reassurance of his "identity crisis". In the lobby of the Lyric, he found Ellison Greer: his physical twin, if a little smaller, and darker skin. Broad forehead, a blade nose, a chin that won the west; and a natural grace, light and bouncy, an aristocrat in a shadowed skin. Yes, it described both of them except for color: Ellison was a butterscotch prince.

They coupled briefly, became deep friends on other levels, conflict never far from hand. And then: murder. After Ellison is found brutally slain, the police were less than helpful. An unusual sex toy seemed the only clue. It's up to Cord to track down the killer. His search for the truth leads through the strangest underworlds New York has to offer. In the police, in his neighbors, in the people who know the truth about that brutal, perverse, modern urban murder, he comes to where the bizarre meets the beautiful – and his very own being is at stake.

> *"The Butterscotch Prince* has my admiration ... a good read in one sitting." — Michael Lynch, *The Body Politic*

> "A deliciously written, softly witty and intricately plotted gay murder mystery ... A delight!" — *In Touch*

Richard Hall's first novel, *The Butterscotch Prince* is a delicious and quirky murder mystery, is newly introduced by Jeffrey Round (*Dan Sharp* mysteries).

The Family of Max Desir
Robert Ferro

It was a family dealing with old values, acceptance and death. Max Desir loved his Italian roots and he loved his American family. As he came of age, Max Desir found love in Italy. Now, at age 40, his American family is split: Max and Nick are accepted as a stable, long-term couple by mother and siblings, but his father John does not. When a needlepoint family tree is to be hung at Christmas, acceptance of family is re-examined. In this beautiful, haunting tale, told in a clear, impassioned narrative, Robert Ferro created a classic. His highly celebrated breakthrough novel is not to be missed.

> "An honest, eloquent and entirely original novel ... at once realistic and mythological, intensely personal and public ... a triumph." — Edmund White

> "Nobody has told this story before, and Robert Ferro has the power to make his telling definitive ... his clear, impassioned narrative moves with wit and sensuous energy. It has shaken and excited me more than any recent American fiction. I want to give it to people. I want everyone to read it." — Walter Clemons

> "A stunning achievement ... not limited to the gay experience, but touches upon the very nature of the human condition ... renews faith in the American novel ... One of the finest (and certainly most moving) novels of the year." — *The Advocate*

Originally published in 1983, this new edition includes a foreword by fellow author and friend Felice Picano.

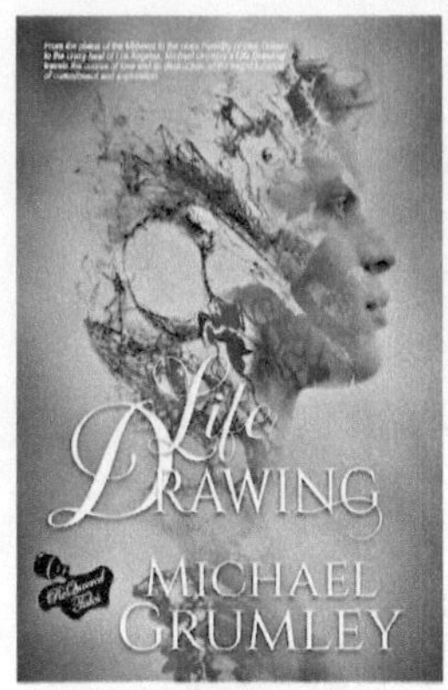

Life Drawing
Michael Grumley

Born in Iowa to the sounds of Bob and Bing Crosby and the Dorsey brothers, Mickey grows up to the comforting images of his living room TV and the reassuring ruts of his parents' life. During the restless summer of his senior year in high school, drifting away from the girlfriend he could never quite love, Mickey spends a night with another boy, and his world will never be the same.

On a barge floating down the Mississippi, he falls in love with James, a black card player from New Orleans, and in time the two of them settle, bristling with sexual intensity, in the French Quarter – until a brief affair destroys James's trust and sends Mickey to the drugs and sordid life of Los Angeles.

"A simple, classic, engaging, and beautifully written tale of a boy who ran away from home, a man who didn't make it in the movies, an artist who found himself earlier than most and did it all west of the Mississippi, in places which, while very American, few Americans have ever been." — Andrew Holleran

"*Life Drawing* affirms the rich complexity of passion in the story of a small-town boy's difficult journey to manhood. Michael Grumley's crisp, direct language brings to life the demanding wonder of sexuality and the delicate tightrope of love between black men and white men." — Melvin Dixon

Originally published in 1991, it was Grumley's only novel, completed in the month's leading to his death from AIDS as he was cared for his lover Robert Ferro. This new edition contains the original foreword by Edmund White (*A Saint from Texas*) and afterword by George Stambolian (*Gay Men's Anthologies Men on Men*), close friends of the couple.

A Perfect Scar and Other Stories
Trebor Healey

This whimsical, sly, and slightly crazy collection of short stories from award-winning novelist, poet, and songwriter Trebor Healey covers much ground. The range is jaw-dropping: from a Vietnamese gangster with a voracious libido and a small boy troubled by his gay dog to an 1870s hermaphrodite cowboy named Captain Jinx ... and then there's the lad who becomes a sex-inspiring satyr, an American Spanish student in Guanajuato seduced by a pair of twins during the Cervantino celebrations, and a housesitting gig that goes terribly awry.

There is humor and insight delivered in lyrical, vibratory phrases, and darker more haunting tales as well, often with a thread of Catholic, as well as Mexican culture, involving young men facing untimely death, reflections on aging, family, duty, sacrifice and sibling rivalry – and the fateful and courageous choices we are forced to make in the name of love.

> "Trebor Healey is all soul ... The way he stacks sentences vibrates on the page. There's an impressive, experimental range in this short story collection. Trebor Healey uses multiple narrators to bring voice to a variety of human experiences."
> — Kirk Read, *How I Learned to Snap*

> "Trebor Healey's writing is suffused with the purest emotion, the bravest, funniest tone, and the perfect balance of poetics, daring and charm." — Joy Nicholson, *The Tribes of Palos Verdes*

Originally published in 2007, this new edition includes a foreword by Peter Dubé (*The Headless Man*).

Boys Like Us
Peter McGehee

Boys Like Us Trilogy, Book 1 – Peter McGehee's debut novel is a rompish, bed-hopping affair – a modern comedy of manners – in which our twenty-something protagonist, Zero MacNoo performs all the rituals – sexual, familial, and grievous – required of urban gay males in the early 1990s. It is a remarkable comedy about life, love, and friendship in the age of AIDS.

Zero, an Arkansas expat who has swapped out Little Rock for the cool cotemporary tones of Toronto gay life, is perplexed by the curveballs of fate. His best friend has been diagnosed with AIDS; Zero is frantic to organize a circle of support. And when Arkansas also calls, it's to support his mother's second marriage and confrontations with the zany array of crazed Southerners he calls family ensue.

> "... a gem of a novel. *Boys Like Us* is funny, sexy, tender, and touching – often in the same sentence." — Larry Duplechan

> "*Boys Like Us* is an affable, enjoyable story ... McGehee has the ability, through an ingratiating style and witty observations, to transform Zero's everyday life into something we care about."
> — Michael Bronski

Funny, bittersweet, outrageous, and moving, Zero's adventures make up the first part of *Boys Like Us* trilogy. This new edition is accompanied by introductions from Dr Raymond-Jean Frontain and long-time collaborator Fiji Robinson.

The Genius of Desire
Brian Bouldrey

Hopelessly drawn to the romantic notion of a double life, young Michael Bellman spends summers in Monsalvat, Michigan, coming of age in a loving tangle of highly eccentric relatives: Great Uncle Jimmy speaks to his dead wife during meals; Cousin Anne torments Michael beyond endurance; reckless Cousin Tommy secretly smokes cigars and can't wait to "kick butt in 'Nam" – and Michael watches every magical move he makes.

A few years and one driver's license later, as family alliances change and long-silent desires surface, Michael begins to understand his attraction to the double life because he's living one – at roadside rest stops, in library washrooms, and public parks. Coming out is the first step, coming to terms is the next ...

> "A simply told story of a young boy growing into manhood and evolving into himself in the midst of the contradictions, deceptions, denial, ignorance, pretensions, confusions, prejudices, and all the other weaknesses that flesh is heir to ... In one way or another this is the same world we must all find our way through and/or out of." — Hubert Selby, Jr. (*Last Exit to Brooklyn*)

A highly praised debut novel in 1993, this new edition includes a foreword by the author.

Winter Eyes
Lev Raphael

A coming-of-age novel set in New York and Michigan during the Vietnam War era, *Winter Eyes* shows how the past controls and divides the immigrant Borowski family, and isolates their American-born son Stefan. But when Stefan comes to learn the terrible secrets at the heart of his family, that knowledge transforms them all and points the way to a happy new future for him, despite his doubts about his sexual identity.

A haunting and remarkable novel, *Winter Eyes* is a tale of family secrets, silence, revelation – and the hope for healing and change. A spellbinding achievement from a talented author of American fiction.

> "Loneliness, separation, desire and the struggle with gay identity are leitmotifs of Lev Raphael's novel. What distinguishes it is Raphael's handling of grand themes, and his ongoing exploration of worlds both Jewish and gay and how they intersect, daring himself and his readers to contemplate wholeness."
> — Jenifer Levin

Lev Raphael is a Lambda Literary Awards winner and multiple nominee for several books. This new edition contains a foreword by Brian Bouldrey (*The Genius of Desire*).

Slashed to Ribbons in Defense of Love
Felice Picano

Felice Picano's first collection of gay short stories spans the period 1975-1982 as published by the pioneering Gay Presses of New York. Read again forty years later, they are a delicious time-capsule of gay life mostly before AIDS and set in iconic gay meccas such as New York and Fire Island. In "Spinning", we get inside the head of a DJ busy spinning for the customers, tricking in his mind and deftly conjuring up the disco subculture which has since faded away. In "The Interrupted Recital", we eavesdrop into the classical music world where ego clashes lead to disastrous outcomes.

There are marvelous character portraits as in "Teddy", about a handsome Vietnam vet back home for a quick furlough. Or the evocation of Christmas in multiple New York households in "Xmas in the Apple". Longer works such as "Hunter", set in a writer's colony, are pure horror fiction. The longest piece, the novella "And Baby Makes Three", spreads its wings recreating Fire Island of the 1970s and features Picano's trademark surprises and miscues which make the tale memorable long after the last page is turned.

> "These stories of love, betrayal, the supernatural, and many other aspects of the human condition, are all waiting for you to explore ... you are about to experience something wonderful." — Eric Andrews-Katz

First published to acclaim in 1982, this new edition features a foreword by Eric Andrews-Katz (*The Jesus Injection*).

Something Inside
Conversations with Gay Fiction Writers
Philip Gambone

In the late-20th century, gay literature had earned a place at the British and American literary tables, spawning its own constellation of important writers and winning a dedicated audience. This collection of probing interviews represents an attempt to offer a group portrait of the most important gay fiction writers.

The extraordinary power of the interviews, originally set down from 1987 to 1997, brings to life the passionate intellect of several voices now stilled among them Joseph Hansen, Allen Barnett, John Preston and Paul Monette. Others such as Scott Heim, Brad Gooch, Lev Raphael, Alan Hollinghurst and Michael Lowanthal were just tasting fame, even notoriety and have gone on to richly deserved acclaim. Published near the height of mainstream accolades for gay fiction as a category, Edmund White, David Plante, Andrew Holleran, Michael Cunningham and Christopher Bram had already enjoyed wide readership and two decades of scrutiny and broad readership.

Many of the pieces are accompanied by portraits from Robert Giard who set out, with urgency during the mid-1980s AIDS crisis, to capture gay artists in their prime; these images make a unique and profound contribution to this collection.

> "A rich collective portrait of some of the most important and interesting gay writers of the last three decades."
> — *Montreal Mirror*

Philip Gambone, a wise and insightful questioner, draws out incredible detail, emotion and personality in a context which still makes for compelling reading thirty years on. The author includes a 2022 update welcoming new readers to this indispensable resource.

$\textbf{\textit{CB}}$

**If you enjoyed this book,
please help spread the word
by posting a short,
constructive review at
your favorite social media site
or book retailer.**

**We thank you, greatly,
for your support.**

And don't be shy! Contact us!

*For more information about current and future releases,
please contact us:*

E-mail: *requeeredtales@gmail.com*
Facebook (Like us!): www.facebook.com/ReQueeredTales
Twitter: @ReQueered
Instagram: www.instagram.com/requeered
Web: www.ReQueeredTales.com
Blog: www.ReQueeredTales.com/blog
Mailing list (Subscribe for latest news): https://bit.ly/RQTJoin

9 781959 902072